COSMIC COLOSSAL

AISHWARYA PANDEY AND FRANCIS A. ANDREW

www.trafford.com
North America & international
toll-free: 1 888 232 4444 (USA & Canada)
fax: 812 355 4082

COSMIC COLLOSAL
Aishwarya Pandey

CONTENTS

Chapter 1

◆
◆ ◆

EXILED TO THE EARTH

She only saw a lonely place, her eyes wide open, and she stumbled towards nowhere.

The pretty girl touched her face. She stared at her hands and was puzzled. Her head was hurt, her hands were extensively bruised, and she was bleeding acutely.

It was a quiet street, and she kept trotting confusedly. She ended up near a crossroad; and hesitated to move on. She glanced around and a cop spotted her.

The girl stopped abruptly. Her face read somewhat odd to the cop. He studied her expressions for sometime and then moved towards her. The girl, too, slowly came up to him.

'Do you need some help?' The cop asked. 'You're bleeding so much! What happened?'

The girl needed help; she needed to know her own name, her purpose, the place, for instance. 'Wha . . . whhat . . . where ami?' she asked him with a blank face.

'What?' the cop said confusedly.

'Who . . .' the girl whispered but then didn't find it useful. She paced away from the cop.

But before anything else could happen, both of them vanished.

However, the girl was the only one to be drawn into a blue path by a mystic force. She was moving fast in that sky blue path with faded white patches all over it. Neither had it clear walls, nor a floor or a ceiling. It was a round and bent tunnel; such that you'd think it terminates after the distant bend. But though the girl had been carried in the path pretty while for now, it was still all the same; no end, same path, same bend and no self control . . . . she had to travel.

However, the tunnel had an end, though the girl never knew where, because a terribly bright white light made her tightly shut her eyes, her hands on her face.

She immediately felt ground under her feet. Loosening her hands from over her face, and opening her eyes, she found a few glowing and divine-looking figures standing in front of her. There was endless dark vicinity and no visible ground. She was in the space, the universe.

There was no air and she couldn't breathe. She began to feel suffocated, while the others stood comfortably. She expected the divine people to help, but what followed revealed that the figures were not-so-divine.

'Welcome.' one of them said to the girl. 'Semester Forthe Visinus. Oh well! Her Mocian ears can't listen to what I say, friends. She can't pick up the fine sound waves of the speech of our kind. These . . . these Mocians can only hear sounds that travel through air-like mediums you know? Can we have some fine adjustment here for this purpose? Oh how I want Semester to hear what I say.'

A swift looking woman at the back, wearing clothes in shades of green like all her fellow ones, came forward and said to the man, 'in no way can she hear us until she has her original body back.'

So Semester, the girl, now had no interest in knowing who she was, what her name was, because she just couldn't breathe. She collapsed on the invisible floor.

'Suffocating?' the supernatural man continued. (pause) 'I think let's bring her to her original self.'

'What?' came a second voice. (though Semester was not listening at all. She was in a desperate condition, but still alive.) 'You mean you'll ask him to give her back her memory, Joz?'

'Oh stop it! That's such a foolish question. We'll never do that. Or who are we to think about it? The lesser she knows, the lesser problems she'd create. Yeah . . . He took her memory out of her mind just for her exile. But even if we've called off the exile, we . . . oh we just can't afford to waste our time in such crude discussions. The officials may trace us. Our protective shields are good and strong, but we ought never to underestimate the officials. I was talking about making her a spirit again.'

(Semester was still alive.)

'Suffocating?' The man asked again. 'But you won't die. You, like us, are a spirit. Spirits don't die; they just end when they are fifty slouts old.' He laughed out loudly and said. 'Slouts? What is that? Little Semester knows nothing!'

The man continued. 'I'll make you the real yourself. This is gonna be how you've always been, except for the few moments you just spent in that tiny planet. Er, Urth.'

'Earth,' someone corrected.

'Oh come on. Let us say Moc de Lilac, why to get confused with silly non-spiritual terms.'

The adjacent woman pulled the sleeves of her shirt and held her wrist where she wore a pink band. She muttered something and a ball of pink light enveloped Semester.

With that, Semester didn't suffocate anymore, though still she wasn't breathing. Breathing was no more a necessity. She too was a divine and glowing spirit now.

Now she looked up slowly, still only a little sign of relief on her face.

'Welcome, Semester Forthe Visinus,' Joz repeated.

Semester could listen now to what he spoke, but she still was perplexed. She wanted to listen now.

'Why are you looking at me girl? Now I am not going to gossip with you. Ok everybody, what next?' the evil spirit continued.

'Talk to Sir about this.' Joz suggested.

'He'll slay us if we disturb him,' another said.

'This is the most important undertaking right now. He'll slay us if the officials rescue this girl.'

'All right,' the other said and went a little aside. He shut his eyes and said something. He seemed to talk to someone.

Such a desperate captivity; Semester didn't know where she was and why she was there. She didn't know her past, had a terrible impression about her present, and was clueless about her future.

Obviously and obnoxiously, neither did she know what a protective shield was nor how it worked. Although she could guess something called Officials were possibly better than the bad spirits that stood in front of her; as we know it : enemy of the enemy—a friend.

Semester decided to speak. 'What's . . .' she said slowly.

'Did you make a sound?' Joz said abruptly before Semester could try to complete. 'Ah, Semester,' he came up to her, 'you haven't yet got a word of what we are talking, right? You know, that's good. And keep it up. Er, you don't have your memories, that's really good. That planet—Moc de Lilac—we just sent you to . . .' He abruptly turned and asked one of his companions, 'Have you burnt that Mocian to nothing? That man who was with this girl before she came here?'

'Yeah.' Came a quick reply.

'All right.' Joz continued. 'So Semester, we exiled you to Moc de Lilac. The Mocians, the people of Moc call it the planet Urth.'

'Earth', someone corrected again.

'Whatever, it's all the same for her. Semester, we have decided to drop the idea of your exile in that planet, but you shouldn't be happy about it. We thought the officials might come to know about you, so we'll now exile you here itself. The suspense will be over in no time.'

'Who are you?' Semester said, angry and frightened.

'Lord! I swear she is really scary,' Joz said and came closer to Semester. He pointed his finger close to Semester's face and warned her, 'take care of the volume and the tone. Don't you show me courage. Not a very appropriate time to do so I think.' Joz said, with a smile that pissed off Semester.

'We have to take her to Location three.' The spirit who was talking to someone with his eyes shut said. 'Joz, you just have to hold the girl firmly and come with us. Just as we'd be about to reach Location three, the guards over there will remove the protective shields of Location three . . . .'

'No.' Joz shouted. 'We will not put the mission to a risk. We'll not put off any shield. A fraction of a moment without a shield and we can be sighted by the officials. We will take her along with the shields to location three.'

He held Semester, who found it pointless to protest. She had got a clear idea of her own helplessness. Everyone gathered around her.

She was lost and invisible amidst their green uniformity. Joz shut his eyes and so did everyone.

Then he said something in a low voice. Things were out of her already small understandable-zone.

Joz tightened his grip on her and said, 'take all of us to Location three.'

This efficiently drove them into the blue tunnel-like path.

Though Semester was much worried about other things, she knew she could use her left hand to cover her face when the bright light would shine. But there was no light this time. They simply reached their destination—Location three.

Location three was a green building surrounded with black fog. (why so green green, Semester wondered.)

On reaching the place, Semester was not given much attention. Joz started talking to the guards. Two others seemed to check the security. Then all of them gathered in the room.

'Leave me.' Semester suddenly shouted, 'I said . . . leave me.'

Every one turned to her.

'All right.' Joz said. 'But, I'm sorry we have to keep the two guards at the entrance . . . Semester, you have to spend the rest of your life in locations like this.'

'Take us to Location four'-and silence. Just the two guards, and Semester.

Semester went to the corner of the room and looked at the green walls. She shut her eyes and said, 'officials . . . Out of location three.'

Nothing happened. She inspected her flawlessly white gown and slowly sat down. She tried again, she shut her eyes and tried going out of Location Three. She spoke each and every word she had heard from Joz and the rest. Every word had been an eye-opener and she remembered everything except her past very well.

'Moc de lilac.' She said, in vain. She sat there wholly-heavy-heartedly. She went out and looked at the guards. They were sincere with there duty. She waited for them to notice her.

She felt it was useless to do anything; I mean to try to do anything.

Cold tears rolled down her divine face.

'Life is a blessing.' A very sweet voice saying lovely words reached Semester's ears. She looked up. It was a beautiful lady with a yellow ring above her head, she had white wings and a violin.

Semester didn't reply.

'When everyone and everything seems against, we are all yours.' The angel said.

Hearing the sound, a guard came in to check. He saw the angel and then Semester and went out.

'He didn't object . . . ?' Semester said in a low voice.

'We are known never to do objectionable things. We treat everyone with love.'

'Can you help me out?' Semester asked.

'We seldom talk. But you are so pretty.' The angel said. 'You are the prettiest girl I ever came across! So I wished to have a word with you. Feel this fragrance.' The angel said and blew her hands softly, Semester felt so refreshed. 'And listen to this music?' the angel said, then playing a fantabulous supernatural tone. All reasons of sadness vanished. Semester smiled.

'Who are you?' Semester asked.

'Ambassador of the God; and also of the God of love, Cupid.' The angel said, with background music. 'We preach that no matter how hard life can go on; it still means life goes on. And when there is not much we can do, we can believe that nature has it; there can not be a universe with only happiness, only love, only comfort, only good. We know good and its contrast both exist, yet it is the good which we must believe in. I will see you later, someone needs me. But I leave with an assurance that things will change.' The angel said, smiling and disappeared.

Instantly, the angel's aura lost its impact.

'Words are easily well spoken.' Semester muttered.

Lonely and upset, Semester felt anger and helplessness combating within her. Positive or negative, she kept thinking, kept thinking . . . .

CHAPTER 2

DAVID'S DILEMMA

Semester remembered nothing, but others did.

Romella was the record holder for being the only friend of Semester with whom Semester had fought only once (and that was even though she was her oldest friend). Romella was tall, had long hair, and a moderately fair complexion. She was a very sober and quiet kind of a girl, and the only child of her parents. But Rodge, Semester's younger and restless brother was treated by her as her sibling; in fact she would be his saviour whenever in a fight Semester would run after his blood.

Romella had not been brilliant in academics, but was assiduous and patient. She was always a good listener and if someone went talking, she would rarely suggest or express anything unless literally asked for it. She was somewhat submissive. All these tempting traits of Romella advocate that in no way could Semester resist her. Romella too considered Semester to be her best friend and no one knew why.

Lastly, Romella was one of the most effected ones when Semester went missing. She was still holding the frames (silver pages that spirits use) of the infolet (newspaper) that told of Semester's disappearance:

Zemezter Forthe Vizinuz 13 mizzing from ze Lilac

Ze popular 13 zloutz old girl with a three word name haz been mizzing from ze Lilac galaxy. It iz to be mentioned that zhe had no criminal chargez againzt her. It iz ze zecond zurprizing event related to her. Yet, ze matter haz not found a place in ze Zenate. However, it iz evident zat it would be talked about in Lilac'z Outer Zenate in ze coming blayz. Meanwhile, ze inveztigation continuez. WHAT IZ ZIZ . . . ??

Romella had gone through these lines a couple of times. She shut her eyes and said, 'talk to David'.

David was the parallel lead of the hazardous David-Semester gang. He was then busy with his work. However, his mind often travelled to Semester's well being. He had always wanted to work in the Government of the Universe. He had been selected for an official's post and the training period was going on. He shut his eyes when Romella called him (via telepathy).

'Hey David.' He saw Romella saying.

'Hey.' David replied, with a mixed reaction.

'David I am worried about Sim. I wonder how her mom and dad are facing this. I did not talk to them. I want to talk to aunt Rose.'

'Yeah do that.' David said.

'I'll do that some other time. Or may be I'll tell my mom to talk to her. Did you talk to anyone?'

'Oh no, I don't know what to talk to them about. I mean I'm sure they're doing their part. Though I'll try to talk to her dad soon, I guess.'

'And did you talk to Rodge?'

'Oh no I didn't . . . Poor chap. Can I handle him in such a crucial time? Romi now you know me, tell me am I a sensible enough person? You got it—no, I'm not.'

'He's just a kid. He'd be so worried. I think he's in Plaryzomes and has not taken any leave. He can't play any role in this case. M . . . just worried.'

'Yeah, me too.' David said. 'But that is not going to help.'

'So . . . What's going on in your mind?'

'So . . . We'll think over it. What do you say?'

'I say that yeah we have to do something. We can't sit back and wait for the officials' response.' Romella began at first.

'Romi. Ya we will,' David said, reconsidering if he was talking to Romella the tongue-tied, 'I know you're worried. But, er . . . right now I am doing some work.'

'Come as soon as possible, then.' Romella said.

'See you, but I don't promise I'll support this whole idea of . . . taking an initiative.' David said, 'what can we plan after all!? It's something that's never happened before! I have no idea!' Ironically, just then an idea came up in David's mind. But he said, 'Do you have an idea?'

'No but we will!'

David sighed. 'But . . . Okay yeah I'll be back and we will talk. I have an assignment. I'll finish it off and will be back. Should I take your job application form as well? Along with me.'

'I'll have a job later on. No, okay you get the form, I'll keep it.'

'Fine, you're confused. Try to relax, Romi. Ya I'll see you soon then Romi. Take care.' David said.

'All right. Then call Justin as well. See ya.' Romella said.

'See ya.' David said and opened his eyes.

Usually David never talked to Romella like this. He loved making fun of her and bantering her. But life was fun sometimes and serious some other times. Anyhow, the idea that had struck him was very much alive in his mind. He looked at his assignment and decided to have a short discussion with Justin.

'Talk to Justin.' He said.

Justin looked even busier. He was holding around four documents in his hands, two under his left arm, and one had just dropped from the grip of his mouth as he said 'ya?'

'Where are you?' David said.

'In the office, dude. I wanted to go to the Outer Senate for the report of the meeting on Semester, but I think I'm not going. Will have to supervise the infolets. What happened?'

'Romella just called up. We wanted to talk on Semester. But I guess you won't be coming.'

'I talked to Semester's dad, you know that?'

'What did uncle say?'

'Oh don't ask man. And aunty, she's so like, upset. I did try to console them.' Justin said, arranging his documents.

'Ahem, console . . . A ray of hope. That's what you look in the middle of the shiny frames you're holding . . . er . . . yeah holding.'

'Happens. When are you guys meeting, and where?' Justin asked.

'I have an assignment right now. You come at Romella's place when you are free, right?'

'That'll be when most of the work is over. But hello, did she . . . hey I'll talk to you later there's some work, guess some reporters are there. I got to goowww . . . .'

David opened his eyes as Justin ran away. He looked at his own assignment. He had the most superb idea for Semester, only that the idea could not be shared.

He got back to doing his work and his mind simultaneously analysed whether he should reveal the secret to Romella and Justin. And finally by the time he finished, he thought that he could.

He went to the Plaryzomes office and got Romella's application form. Then he shut his eyes and said, 'Romella's place'.

The blue path did carry him to Romella's place. It was the most commonly used transport, known as the "Quixie Flier"; and for any spirit who had her or his memories safe with them, it was not mysterious.

When David was in front of Romella's house, he did not stand there for long to think any more and went inside.

'Romi', he said that he had come. He was the tallest of all the four friends. He had black eyes and sharp features. He had an attractive personality and was manipulative, ambitious, jovial and daring; (and handsome).

'Hi.' Romella replied. 'Sit.'

Romella's house was a typical, lower middle class type. Its iron walls had no added decorative to overshadow its grey look.

David straightaway went ahead, sat on a chair and said 'Er . . . So, are you sure . . . I mean . . . How are you?'

'I'm fine.' Romella said as she seated herself on another cubical chair. 'How are you? Everything fine?' She spotted the application form but didn't ask for it.

'Ya I'm fine. Should we go out or we'll just talk here. I mean do you want an outing or something?'

'Oh no. Not toblay.' Romella said with a smile. 'Where's Justin?'

'He'll be here.' David said. 'By the time he does, Romi tell me shall we not wait for the Senate meeting, I mean the matter is already in the Outer Senate. Are you sure you are not, I mean, letting the officials do it?'

'Is this David who is saying this!? Were all your adventurous instincts a fake? I'm not saying the officials are definite to fail,' Romella grabbed the topic. 'Things like this have happened in our life. And we have always tried to solve them! Let the . . .'

'Things like this have-not-happened.' David interrupted. 'You can't compare the previous issues to this one.'

David got up and picked the infolet kept on the iron table near the front door, putting the application form there instead.

He read out from the infolet, 'It is one of the most surprising events which emerged in the near history . . . it would be talked about in Lilac's Outer Senate in the coming blays . . . Look. It is different.'

'And it was different for us when we fought danger for the first time? It's always different every time you start doing something new, David. When you started walking, for example.'

'Hmm. Okay but this time I really don't think we can . . . hang on actually, we can do something.' David said with a constantly dying volume.

'What?' Romella responded with a reflex.

David looked here and there and hesitated to start at once.

'What David?' Romella leaned forward as if a detective had found a murder mystery's strongest link. 'And do you think you don't need to do anything 'cause you are safe? Mind you David, you were not safe anytime when anyone of us was in danger. We four have been safe or in danger together.'

'It's not like that.' David said, taken aback by Romella's new incarnation.

'Why? How can you say that? Tell me one big thing which did not happen to all four of us together.'

'That is exactly what I am finding hard to tell you.'

'You are an idiot.' Romella said, in a lower voice.

'Wooh. You are fine, for sure, right? And silly, you'll find one or the other big thing having had happened to every next spirit. I agree we four had really shocking incidents but something big happened just to me and Sim.' David said. 'Shit! I had thought I'd tell you but . . . shit I shouldn't have said it.'

'What big thing? What are you saying?' Romella asked,

'I can't,' David said, looking distressed.

'Are you sure? Look; me and Justin know everything.' Romella said.

'No. You don't.' David said, looking firmly into Romella's eyes.

'Hello! You said it would help Semester! There is no point, heck! You have to tell!' looking as restless as a deserving officer would look on denial of promotion.

'Have to?'

'Are you insane? Of course! What else.'

'Oh please I request you don't do that. I'll be in a great dilemma. And you, Romi, there's no use of telling you! You can hardly help your own self.'

Romella got back to her normal self and made a face that demanded so much pity.

While David found this face was more on the funny side, he controlled his emotions and said, 'try to understand Romi, I can't help it because I can't. It'll be unethical. It's not just a big thing that happened to me and Sim. It is the biggest thing that could happen. You can't . . . .'

'Even if it costs you Semester? What big-big are you talking about? And why did you come here?' Romella asked with big eyes.

'Because I wish we could find some other way.' David explained.

'Cool.' Romella said and there was silence. 'Think.'

David shut his eyes and touched his forehead; again his mind started analysing whether he should tell Romella. He opened his eyes and said, 'trust me, Romella. And it's not that I think I am safe, so why get into danger. Not that I fear. Trust that I really can't tell it to you like that. Really.'

'Ya I said it's cool.' Romella said, looking humiliated. 'Where's Justin?'

'When I talked to him he was busy. But he said he had talked to uncle.'

'Uncle Peter?'

'Yeah. They both are worried like . . . you can understand.' David said.

'What else did uncle say?'

'Not much. That's what Justin told. He said he would come after the Outer Senate meeting gets over and the news for the infolets is arranged.' He shut his eyes and said, 'Talk to Justin.'

Romella, meanwhile guessed David's secret, feeling bad that even Semester did not tell her a big thing.

'He is shielded. Must be still busy,' David said.

'I can't guess what is that biiig thing you both only share. And so I can't imagine it can help Semester right now. But I guess I just know that when the sadness is full right from your top upto your toes, you'll forget everything and be as daring as ever, you will tell it.'

David mentally mocked this dialogue of Romella's which was supposedly meant to be an emotional black-mail.

But Romella knew her friends very well, she generally could tell how they would react to a particular situation. David did not express anything on this latest prediction of hers, but he was afraid Romella was right.

Justin was actually yet not free. He had tried very hard and finally he was one of the crew members from the Infolet Department that were allowed to be present at the Outer Senate's meeting. The Outer Senate of the Lilac galaxy, which is at the centre of it, I mean The Milky Way, was now ready for the meeting. The Head, Sir Lilac, was just going to enter the meeting room.

The Outer Senates deserve a description by now, positively. They are the residences of the Heads of their respective galaxies. The Head is the superior most official in a galaxy and the Head is named after the name of the galaxy, as simple as that. The name of the head is the name of the galaxy itself. The Outer Senate of the Lilac was basically similar to all the other Outer Senates; their basic code being that the building should be made of gold, and only green stones like the emeralds could be used for the beautification. The colour code of most of the other things is also green such that ultimately it is essentially golden and green. In totality, it is not something that can be imagined until it is actually visited.

The grandeur of the building is impressive, amazing, divine, tempting, luxurious, captivating but yet not unbeatable, because there is also the Senate, where the Master of the Universe resides. Unlike the Heads of galaxies, the Master does not have to change his name for his post. (Master does not account for gender discrimination, but as a matter of fact, there had never been a Mistress of the Universe). The Senate is the superior most office in the universe, and unbeatable; and it will be talked about later.

Well, the stunning Outer Senate of the Lilac galaxy was stunned for the time being, as a spirit native to the galaxy was missing. The

Head, Sir Lilac, entered the room with two attendants on either side, and got himself seated at the central chair. Then all the officials, except the Head took out the pink bands they were wearing on their wrists and put them in front of them on the big table.

'I thank you for the respect.' The Head began with a not-very-thankful tone. 'Let the discussion begin.'

The official of the Infolet Department officially introduced the matter to the Outer Senate. As he spoke about Semester's birth star, that is, the star of which she was the spirit, her famous three word name, her education, her previous records and her disappearance, the appointments kept jolting down the points on the official frames.

'. . . It has been two blays that Semester Forthe Visinus 13 has not been heard from. The meeting must now proceed towards its purpose.'

'The Investigation Officer,' Lilac said.

An official on Lilac's left opened his papers and read, 'Sir and fellow members, it is as follows. Yesterblay, on her parents' notice, the check revealed that Semester 13 is not present. She could not be seen, contacted or reached at. The investigation revealed that her last pictures were only available till two blays prior to now. She, herself had locked her pictures, in other words, shielded herself, at her home and that is her last video available. Here it is projected.'

An appointment bowed to Lilac with his pink band on the top of his hands and said, 'May I?'

'You may.' Lilac answered.

The appointment wore his band and projected Semester's last video on the front wall.

Semester, with lesser confusion seen on her face, was at her home. Her back door could be seen and she was sitting on a table. She was not looking worried or tensed, but nor did she look cool and perfectly okay. She had a pink band on her wrist and she was wearing a pink gown. She shut her eyes and said, 'Shield to all levels.' With that, there was no more any projection on the wall. The appointment took out his band.

The official continued. 'Next, I am presenting the current conclusions and possibilities we have reached. It was revealed that she had shielded herself two more times before this. This indicates her self involvement in the matter. However, since if a spirit shields herself or himself, it can still be known which galaxy she or he is in; but as of now, nothing can be known about Miss Semester 13. The legal definition of 'missing' refers exactly this. So, Semester is missing.'

He paused and turned over the page. 'It is possible that she did not want to be traced and so she asked someone else to shield for her; so that her location could not be traced at all. We have checked the videos of the seven spirits she was closest to, the eight hundred two spirits she knew, and the eight thousand six hundred sixty nine spirits she had ever met, but it is contradictory that none of them has created a shield for someone else in the time period. In other words, none of them have shielded Semester. In fact only one of her friends named Master Justin 13, who's in the Infolet Department had been shielded recently, and that was for reasons regarding the security of the news, we have checked it thoroughly. The checking for many others continues. Surely, we are taking the case with responsibility and goodwill. There are no criminal records the girl holds. Thank you.'

'The next orders are?' Sir Lilac said.

Another official, with a face that reminded of a disfigured pumpkin said, 'Sir. Due to the shields, Semester is actually isolated from our investigations. Links are what we are concentrating on. The next orders given are; continuing the checking of spirits who might have shielded her. All-time direct links to Semester are important such that just in case she can be reached at, we don't miss it. That is to say, if she is even momentarily without her shields, it won't remain unnoticed. Also, it is ordered to observe thoroughly early videos of all the seven spirits who were closest to her, as it is possible they had discussed it with Semester. Thank you.'

'Thank you?' Lilac said. 'Those orders are not sufficient.'

For sometime, no one in the room spoke. Then Lilac said, 'to add to the orders, let Semester's residence be searched. Moreover, in case Semester returns on her own, she will be viable for being punished on grounds of creating great instability. The next meeting will not take place until two blays. Thank you.'

Lilac stood up and the others also followed. He was escorted away from the meeting. The appointments handed over the jolted points to the Editing Officer while the reporters and others related to the news, including Justin, still waited in the last room to get the edited news. Well, the infolets would not have plenty to inform.

CHAPTER 3

THE SECRET LIFE

The enmity Semester had with her kidnappers had a high profile. A famous hateful incident was very much related to David and Semester.

Whenever legally important, a spirit is ended by the government before he or she has completed the otherwise fixed fifty slouts of age. This procedure requires the consent of at least a thousand Heads who vote for it. In case the Master of the Universe also agrees, he is equivalent to a hundred votes. Though this is not a very usual procedure, it had recently occurred two slouts ago. Surprisingly, the Master of the Universe himself was the criminal. His name was Zolahart. He had tainted his powers and operated a secret elite group that worked under him. Just as Zolahart became the first master in the huge history to be displaced from the Master's post, David and Semester had accidentally dropped in front of him but luckily escaped. Zolahart had then shielded himself and created havoc. Along with his followers, he attacked spirits and tried to invade the Outer Senates and the Senate.

All this had forced the government to call an emergency meeting. Not only thousand, but a swarming number of Heads were in favour of ending Zolahart.

The Fireball of Power was a glowing ball that had existed since as long as the government had. It was used by senior officials for taking oaths; and by the volunteering officials for the procedure of ending a spirit; indifferent to the presence of the concerned criminal spirit in the showground.

Zolahart was legally ended soon, implying an end to the attacks.

This hateful incident was very much related to David and Semester.

The small things Semester no more recalls are like this; she is native to the Lilac galaxy, an active and all rounder beautiful girl. She was initially very much like her father and very different from her mother. Her mother, Rose, was an extremely sentimental, tolerant and caring woman. By this I mean that she would neglect her discomfort and problems to do good to others; and that she could tolerate very hard times, just in the hope that her kids will change her life sometime. She had very laboriously brought up Semester, and Semester had always made her proud by her talent in academics, creativity, show-offs etc. But technically, Semester was just a normal spirit for quite a long time (only that she was extraordinarily pretty always).

The spirits don't get educated, they get experated; and the educators are known as experators. The Atz galaxy, or as we Mocians call it—the Andromeda, is the nearest one to Semester's native Lilac galaxy.

Rose was an experator in Iliaegazomes, the institute of spiritual learning of the Lilac galaxy, while Semester had got her experience, from Plaryzomes, the institute of spiritual learning in the Atz.

Her parents had faced enormous difficulty in leaving her at the institute for the first time. Semester would simply not let go of her mother and not even the staff members could convince her. Then finally when she attended a class, she slid over the floor from behind the other students and ran away. The other students could only understand by the time she had left. As they brought it to the notice of the experator, Semester picked up speed. Without thinking, she ran to the Chief Experator's office where she by chance found her mother's friend. Then she cried until her experator came searching for her all the way from the classroom and convinced her back to the class.

Very soon Semester made her first friend Romella. That was perhaps because Semester talked a-lot, and there was no better listener around than Romella. David and Justin joined them not so early. In fact Romella was reluctant to be friends with them. David enjoyed teasing Romella and he fancied the way Romella made a baby face and a squeaky sound. But David hardly made fun of

Semester and so Semester explained to Romella that she shouldn't mind small jokes. She handled both the parties and later all the four got accustomed to living together.

Romella secretly didn't like sharing Semester with anyone, but so what; Semester never asked her what she liked. Also, Semester was actually crazy. She could cross limits for fun, and David was just like a blessing from the heavens as a partner for such activities. Breaking rules was probably the first rule in their life. Adventures greatly fascinated them and the activities which made people say things like 'Are you mad?' 'No, I'm not joining in', 'Wow, that's cool' were her favourites. She had no belief in following what everyone did.

'Live for fifty slouts and then off you go.' She often repeated her pet dialogue. 'What's the use? Be famous! In fact, be different . . .'

Sometimes she would be replied, 'You have a different three-word name.'

'Name? How many know about it. I'd better have a quarter-word name but a famous one. Even I don't know why I have such a long name.' Semester would say.

David was not less daring. Justin loved books and Romella, well her only fault was that she was not adventurous. So David and Semester left them often, shielded themselves and went out to strange places and many a times faced danger. They also slipped into the 'Prohibited Plaryzomes Lab' when they had nowhere else to go. The most attractive things there were the prohibited instruments, and the well-arranged system waiting to get tempered with. To other students David and Semester's disruptions soon became normal. Many a times they were tempted to enjoy with David and Semester, but they never did. The experators were too fed up of complaints. Though the Plaryzomes Chief Experator—Sir Laurins had many tasks to be done, one of them was essentially dealing with the side-effects of David-Semester combo.

Once like every time, David and Semester had escaped Plaryzomes. They went to the outskirts of the Atz, shut their eyes and said, 'take us to the nearest place where we can be thrilled.'

They had done it many a times. Once they had reached Chief Experator Laurins's house; another time they had magically appeared onto a stage where some kids were performing a stage show 'NO MAGIC'.

Though, this time they never knew it was going to be an event of a lifetime. They were living their last moments of being 'normal'.

Zolahart had always wanted to harm Semester, but everyone thought it was this incident that made her his enemy.

Zolahart was then the master of the Universe. He was standing outside one of his personal buildings talking to someone with his eyes shut. His building was shielded to all levels and so was not visible in any case. But Zolahart, himself was out of the building and had only shielded his conversation and videos. When Semester and David dropped in front of him, they could see him. They were awestruck to see the Master of the Universe in front of them.

Semester was glad and David was a little surprised. David that moment inaugurated his pet reaction, he said, 'this is not real.'

Zolahart opened his eyes when he heard the sound. He went furious and said, 'you heard everything'.

'What?' Semester said, confused at the expressions on Zolahart's face, 'Sir . . . We heard nothing. We just . . .'

'Go to hell.' Zolahart shouted. Semester and David saw that Zolahart did not have a pink band on his wrist, but a black one. He attacked them before they could understand what's going on.

Zolahart shut his eyes and so did David immediately. 'Take to Plaryzomes' David shouted and could hear Zolahart saying something but they luckily went off by the Quixie flier.

When they reached Plaryzomes they were still in a state of shock. They thought they'd immediately tell the Plaryzomes staff about it, but instead the students encircled round them and stunned them by what they told.

'I told you not to go out.'

'Breaking news—the Master is wanted by the government.'

'He is a criminal!' Justin shook David.

David opened his mouth to say something but no sound came out. He looked at Semester.

"His spell worked!" Semester wanted to say, but she could not speak either. The students finally got shocked as well.

The time that followed was not the kind of adventurous Semester and David would have liked. They were banned from going out of Plaryzomes and the only way that could be made possible was by impounding their bands, they were given protection as Zolahart could still have been after them. Their parents also had loads of lectures to be imparted.

'Huh!' Semester's reaction behind her parents went like this, 'that's fake. To scare us.'

'Why? Don't you want to get withdrawn from Plaryzomes?' Romella asked.

However, David agreed to Semester, 'oh no I know they'll not do anything further. We should be awarded! I tell you. Not black-mailed. (pause) That man rocked the universe but not us. Hi-five?'

'Hi-five!' Semester cheered David up, 'that was cool. You have to agree.'

After a small and un-restful time period, everything got back to normal when the infolets informed everyone that Zolahart was ultimately legally ended by the officials.

'Had I been late by a moment, we were gone.' David said.

'How?' Semester asked, not ready to let David feel superior.

'Mind it. He made us "dumb"! Had I been a little, a little late in bringing us to Plaryzomes, neither of us would have been able to utter "take us back"; we would have remained dumb for a lifetime.'

'I strongly support you.' Justin said from behind his book, just in order to shut David up.

'Ya.' Semester said. 'But it was you idiot who opened his mouth and said this is not real!'

'As if had I not said anything, we would have sneakily slipped away. And what did you want me to do anyway? Listen to him until he was over with his conversation? And then when he would open his eyes, I'd say, we have heard your great evil plans. By the way, sir, this girl standing next to me is a great fan of yours. Take her along with you. She has always wanted to be famous.'

'Haenh . . . very funny.' Semester made a face. 'Let's go.' She held Romella's hand and Romella went in whichever direction Semester pulled her.

The two girls went towards the playground. Semester said, 'Oh well thank god David said that in time.'

'Why don't you say thanks to him then?' Romella said, smiling.

'I have said it.' Semester told. 'But it's not a prayer that has to be repeated every next blay. Do I have to worship him now?'

'Don't go out of Plaryzomes like that next time.' Romella said.

'You're right, I can't. We're banned.'

'Don't go even when you'll be allowed.'

'You want me to bore myself deliberately? I can't torture myself,' Semester said. 'Zolahart has been put to an end,' she said sitting on an experator's chair, 'and there's a lot I've yet not tried.'

Semester was very wrong to talk like that. One, because she knew that no one was going to let her easily wander anymore, and secondly because Zolahart was still very much alive.

Though his real face had been exposed, but exposed too late. His magical powers had merged with his devil instinct and will power; he could do things like remaining alive even after he was thought to have been ended. Why not I say in short—he was eternal.

He had grown into a ferocious master whose expanded circuit now included some active officials.

It was the building outside which David and Semester had first confronted him that was later renamed to Location three, Semester's lockup.

CHAPTER 4

◆
◆ ◆

ZOLAHART'S REASON TO CELEBRATE

Semester had been in Location three for one blay; totally idle. She was hopeful that time would change; but the new guards at the duty were the only change in her life.

Loss of memory choked her; it was terrible to be so blank.

She thought she should have a pink band. In fact, all the time she kept thinking what all she should have.

She was still busy thinking when she heard some movements outside. She glanced from the edge of the door and saw Joz with a few familiar and a few unfamiliar spirits. Some of them noticed her. She believed it was crucial to talk to them, otherwise it'd mean another long wait to see them again.

'Please.' Semester stepped out saying loud and clear. 'I don't like it.'

'If we thought you liked it, we would have never put you here.' Joz said.

Semester's ego suddenly overcame her and she ran towards Joz. A woman who stopped her and Semester immediately caught hold of her wrist, where her hand could touch the pink band. Joz held his own band without delay and muttered something that threw Semester away.

Semester got up and headed towards Joz again.

'Do whatever you want to do with her.' Joz told the guards. 'We have more to do than playing.'

All of them shut their eyes and disappeared.

One of the guards threw her straight into the room, banging her on to whatever came on her way.

'Damn you.' Semester shouted from inside, with her grave combination of tears and rage. 'You think you are that good. It's the band that is. Take it off or give it to me and then you watch out.'

Zolahart was now at the deadline of his age, he was nearly fifty; but he looked full of youth and energy; and ambitions.

He had many locations for various purposes, all green with black fog around. However, his residence was Location one.

The meeting at the Outer Senate had merely been a formality; and Zolahart was going to hold his own meeting at Location two.

Flying from Location three after he attacked Semester, Joz had reached the venue of the meeting. All the invitees had not reached yet, nor had Zolahart. Everyone present there was waiting in what they called the waiting room, because Zolahart always made them to wait.

Everyone waited for pretty long and discussed about certain plans that they could present to the Master. There were also speculations about his heir, as he was nearing his natural end. Slowly they started moving into the main hall of the building. The ten guards remained quiet and sincere at the gate.

Inside the hall, there was essentially silent atmosphere. Without any announcement, Zolahart arrived with six guards. Though having guards was nothing more than a show-off to him. He was floating above the invisible ground. He veered and hovered inside. Part of his black outfit flowed behind him like a long cloak. His eyes reflected superiority and seriousness. His hair was not very tidy. His face had an unusual green complexion. There was not a sign of weakness though he was just a little less than the age when a spirit naturally ends. He had jet black hair and not grey. He had one round mark near his throat since the very time the officials had, according to them, legally ended him.

Everyone stood up. Just one look at Zolahart's face, and all the plans they had discussed seemed zero.

He turned around with style and seated himself on a huge rigid sofa, covering the whole of it. His hands were rested in such a way that they conveyed fearlessness, and also exposed his black band. Everyone settled down.

There was pin-drop silence and the guards then moved out.

'How's that girl?' Zolahart thundered and his voice filled the aura.

Two spirits gathered the courage to reply and began together. 'She . . .'

The two exchanged looks spontaneously and one of them went silent. The other continued. 'Semester is a waste. There's no need to worry, Sir.'

'Of course.' Zolahart said. 'The timid officials. The petty Head . . . Lilac. And an undeserving new Master of the Universe.' A smile ran over his face, full of disrespect. 'Next, get that boy. Dayvid. Just get him.'

Everyone nodded in agreement.

'I have always been the master!' He thundered. 'And I will get it back. It'll all be under me. This is not a meeting, I must say, it is a celebration.'

All the invitees wished to exchange dumb looks, but they did not move their heads.

'Soon I will achieve what no one would have dreamt of, thought of. You all have worked hard. You all want power, and you will get it under me.

Suddenly, Zolahart's eyes xecuti on one man. 'Who are you?' Zolahart asked with a clear false patience.

'I . . . I Sir . . . was . . . told to . . . . to . . .'

'Were you told to come here?' Zolahart asked.

'Sir . . . I can . . .'

'Were you told to come here?' Zolahart said softly, putting his hand on his black band. 'It's a one word answer.'

'No . . . ssss . . .'

Zolahart held his band and with a jerk, lifted the man up, though still below his level. With another jerk, Zolahart hit the man's head on the floor. As the others kept watching like dumb audiences, Zolahart kept hitting the man until his face lost its design. His face had blue blood all over it. He was just alive but better dead. The rest all witnessed this with big eyes and no movement.

'I require only the few Zolharites to be present here, whom I have handpicked to be present. Take him away and throw him somewhere in a location.' Zolahart ordered and two workers immediately obeyed. The man kept murmuring for mercy, but one could not even guess where on his disfigured head the sound was coming from.

The invited faithfuls slowly turned back to Zolahart. They gulped fearing that they might have unknowingly done a small mistake which could take them from the honoured elite group to a tortured petite group.

'Where is the guard who let him inside?' Zolahart inquired.

'No, I didn't even know this man was here. Yeah.' Joz consoled himself.

After some hesitation, two women brought in two guards, one of whom looked like a wax statue.

'Do the same to them and take them away.' Zolahart said.

The women dragged them out but none of them dared to protest at all while being taken out.

Zolahart announced, 'Mind it my dear ones, mistakes are not welcomed. But are you afraid of me?'

Everyone wondered how they should react to this question. The answer was definitely yes, but the might have had to be no.

'N—no . . .' A gutsy lady from the end of the second row stammered.

Zolahart was facing the other side. He didn't move for a moment or two, and then turned in a reflex and green light blew out of his band. It hit the lady and she flung to the wall and fell down and lost her conscience.

'I hope that will scare her a bit.' Zolahart said, comfortably seating himself, with a smile. 'Who are you going to be afraid of, if not me? But you all have no more choice left. You have made your choice now. And all you have left to do is to enjoy power. Anyone who ever tries to change his or her mind, I'll change your life.'

Everyone stood up and bowed as Zolahart left his seat and then continued, 'After becoming the first one, who is great enough to have outlived a . . . . leegal xecution!' Zolahart started laughing oddly and the audience prayed he would quieten up as soon as possible because they didn't have the alternative choice of stopping their ears. 'I am going to become the first one to outlive a bloody span of fifty slouts of fixed tiny age (the wanna be heirs gulped). This is probably the first and last celebration, the one demarcating the beginning of a legendry embarking. This is not to entertain you, but to remind you of the luxury, and of this being the last time you can behave this way, of course in my absence.'

Zolahart floated above all of them toward the exit. Everyone got up and cheered for him as he passed by and out of the location.

Thirty spirits appeared and the sky of Location two filled with fireworks and blasts and everyone cheered. More workers walked in with beverages of dozens of kinds. The foods and delicacies were arranged orderly along a side wall and were not meant for being eaten. In fact, they were not supposed to be touched. They were decoratives.

The meeting at Location two was completely different from the one at the Outer Senate. It had no rules, no transparency, and there was wildness all around.

The blackness of the fog, the green colour of the location and the fear hid for sometime in the light of the beautiful fireworks and the cheers.

CHAPTER 5

THE FINAL THINGS

Justin reached David's home late on the next blay of the Outer Senate's meeting, holding an infolet. David had left his door open.

'I knew you'd be at home.' Justin said, his eyes then dropped down to David's clothes. David was wearing a formal outfit. 'And I would have been wrong if I was a bit late.'

'Why?' David said 'Hey get in. I just came back from work. It took a long time toblay. I'll just change, wait.'

'Okay then I would have been wrong if I came a bit early . . .' Justin muttered. 'Don't change what you're wearing! We are going out.'

'Where?'

'Romi and you met yesterblay.' Justin explained. 'But I couldn't come. I want both of us to go there. Now.'

'Er . . . please no . . . Justin.' David said.

'?' Justin was taken aback.

'I mean Romella is . . . there's nothing actually that we can talk to her about. Er . . . you can talk to me here.'

Justin gave a blank look and spread his hands in front of him as a sign of 'What?'

'I mean . . . oh come on she's a girl. We should not trouble her. She'll get upset, you know.'

'Oh, right.' Justin said. 'Yes she is a very girly girl.'

'Hey I told you I talked to Sim's dad.'

'Oh right. You were going to tell me.' David said, drinking his favourite Swail non-veg soup and not asking Justin for it.

'What would he. I had just called to tell him I care.' Justin said. 'At times like this everyone knows everybody feels almost simimlarly, so we didn't have many words to say. He was busy. You crook.' Justinn said as David finished the soup in front of his eyes.'

'What impressed me was that he's always so focussed.' Justin continued. 'So, you must have read the latest infolet?'

'No . . . I just got back I told you. I was just going to-'

'Okay. You go and change.' Justin said.

'M fine.' David said, snatching the infolet from Justin and hunted for the information concerned.

Zemezter'z rezidence be zearched: Zir Lilac

Ze Outer Zenate meeting began with ze reportz zat everyone Zemezter knew waz under inveztigation. Zir Lilac found ze orderz were not enough and he told Zemezter'z rezidence be zearched. Zemezter'z lazt video revealed zat Zemezter had zhielded herzelf to all levelz on her own. Alzo, officer Makken told ze meeting zat Zemezter waz actually mizzing becauze it can not be even known in which galaxy zhe iz; which indicatez zat now zomeone elze haz zhielded her. A pozzibilty iz zat Zemezter told zomeone elze to zhield her. Zir Lilac zaid if Zemezter came back on her own, zhe will be viable for being punizhed for creating inztability. No meeting would be held for two blayz az ordered, until emergency. Much information was not made public. Ze order by ze end was merely to continue ze inveztigationz.

'What the hell?' David said. 'Why would she ask someone else to shield for her if she has not even discussed it with us or her parents?'

'Point.' Justin said. 'But who can reach her and shield her without her knowing about it? She had already shielded herself. So I am almost sure she asked someone to do it.' Justin paused and raised one of his eyebrows. 'And I guess we all are sure none of us has done it?'

'Oh come on.' David said. 'M worried about her. And so is Romi, and her parents.' He raised his left eyebrow and said. 'And I guess you are also worried, coz you don't know where she is?'

'What? Of course I don't know where she is!' Justin said. 'I don't get free from the office but that doesn't mean m not worried, man.'

'Well, Justin,' David muttered. 'I'll call Romella here.'

'Now suddenly you need Romella to the rescue?' Justin said.

In no time, the three were sitting around a small table gravely.

'Don't make such faces.' David said, not knowing that Joz's army of hundred, as ordered by Zolahart, was ready to approach his house. All they wanted was David, as ordered by Zolahart.

'You both, I mean me as well; we can do something.' David continued.'

'Only if you end the suspense.' Justin said.

David opened his mouth to say something but didn't. Justin and Romella were staring at him as if he was wrapped in a cuisine. And Zolahart's men and women lead by Joz reached near the house.

'All right.' David said. 'We are here to talk on what we can do to find Semester.' He shut his eyes and said 'Shield us and this house to all levels.'

'Damn. Where did it go.' Joz shouted as the house vanished in front of his eyes.

'Where's the house. We want that boy!' A gigantic woman said.

As a pink shield appeared and faded off, Justin and Romella said together 'What have you done?'

'Our videos are under observation' Justin continued 'and right now the officials must be thinking that we are with Semester.'

'If you ask me,' Romella squeaked, 'I don't like adventures that get me into problems, adventures of . . .'

But probably no one had asked her for views. 'And . . . okay . . . my mom and dad can stay somewhere else for the time being.' David said. 'We will be shielded now until we find Semester.'

'What? For probably the rest of our life?' Justin said.

'May I speak now?' David said, looking frustrated. 'I know who can save Semester.'

'What?' Romella jumped while Justin responded late with a 'Who?'

'Yes.' David continued. 'It's the one who we know as the God.'

'This can't be happening dude you are crazy!' Justin said, disgusted. 'I have heard many say this. God alone can save Semester.'

'I'm not talking about that God in poems you understand?' David shouted. 'I'm talking about the one who was the first spirit billions of trillions of slouts ago. The creator of this and that and me and you. The creator of all the magic, spirits, non spiritual creatures, and the most powerful of all times. Sir Paradis.'

Romella and Justin had been listening to David now like a demon had entered their best friend.

'Woh . . .' Justin said, a little scared. 'You are mad with grief. That's all I say.'

David instead turned to Romella. 'It is that big thing that I couldn't tell you Romi.'

Now Romella could believe David more than Justin could.

'But you said something had happened to you both?' she asked.

'We had met the God.' David announced.

'I'll just be back from the washroom.' Justin said. He got up and said to David, 'When I'll be back, you make sure you don't tell me things like this if it's a joke. Cause it's not funny.'

After they all were convinced, David began with how it had happened.

'When it happened, I was a hundred times more shocked than you are right now, and so was Sim. It was just around a fifty blays before we had come across Zolahart. You may think that the Zolahart incident was the only incident that happened to us which could make headlines, but actually this one would . . . But it was unethical to reveal it and so we never . . .'

'Just tell me how it happened!' Justin slapped David and said.

'Yeah . . .' David said, touching his cheek. 'We had gone on . . . one of our usual adventures. You remember that blay when you had issued a book from the library and I had dropped it ten storeys below and . . . .'

'I don't.' Justin held David by his collars and shook him.

'Stop it.' Romella said, pulling Justin back. 'And David, just shut up and tell us how did it happen?'

'Ya, but I need to explain. And let me do it the way I want.' David said, shoving away Justin's hands. 'We were near a beautiful nebula, trying to take a little risk. Sim found out it was a hot nebula and she challenged me to get to its centre. She threw light on it, yes she could do that, that's her indigenous magic . . . and it reflected marvellous red light. Our adventure started. She kept throwing light to create special effects and I flew inside, very fast. It was amazing and thrilling to decide which way would be safer. The intensity of the red light the nebula was reflecting helped me to know which way would be less denser. I had hardly even entered it properly, when the nebula started getting too dense and I couldn't any more find safe way to the inside. I started flying back, and that was as difficult as it had been coming inside. I was just trying to take a quick bend when I found yellow light all around and I couldn't guess where I was. I was slowing down though it wasn't me who was doing it. Though I didn't feel any heat so I thought I'm not falling into one of its hot-spot or somewhere dangerous. But soon I found I'm not able to get out, I had no idea where I was or whatever. Now I got nervous. It felt like being lost in a yellow cloud. I called for Semester but I was far away from her. I shut my eyes and said 'Take me to Semester.' But nothing happened. I said it again. But yet, no use. I was panicking, kind of, when to my relief Sim appeared in front of me and asked what had happened. She noticed the strange yellow thing around us and held my hand and said, what is this, this is strange. Then she too shut her eyes and said 'Take us out of here.' But, it was no better. We are trapped, I told her. We were worried. We would not actually feel any danger but things just looked dangerous. Then slowly we noticed the yellowness got pale. Sim showed me from where the rays were coming. Something tiny was lying at a small distance and we could see a number of individual yellow rays emanating . . . the rays soon finished off, and the yellowness around us had also gone. We saw that the rays had reduced to a frame, an old withered frame, a yellow one. We had only seen silver sheets yet, a golden page, it was new to us. We started feeling hot pretty soon and we recalled we are inside the nebula. I picked up the frame and then we immediately got out, we could get out this time.'

'Was something written on it? Where's the frame now?' Justin interrupted again.

'It's not with me. Sim had taken it and I don't know what she did with it. It's been pretty long.'

'You can't call it a frame.' Justin said factually. 'A frame has to be a very normal paper of silver.'

'Let's have a group discussion on it.' David said, sarcastically.

'Er . . . What then? What was written on that old-and-withered paper, ya, that was it.' Justin said.

Romella didn't speak. She was lost in the story.

David continued. 'Once we were out, we didn't chat, we simply read what was written on it, we had to ensure it was not a problem carrying that frame. The page read odd language. Thou move to the maximum in which direction the rays did reduce to bear this; its an order blah blah . . . We made out that it told us where to go. But we couldn't decide why we should go somewhere on an unknown's order. And who the hell can order us like that anyway? But it was an adventure, and tempting first of all. We had not been harmed so far, so, we of course decided to go. We shielded ourselves for protection, and went. On reaching there we found nothing for sometime. But soon we found a figure appear on our front and a yellow shield around us. When the figure got clear we saw who was standing there. Sir Paradis! Sim sounded mesmerized saying that. And, well, I said, this is not real. But Sim was awestruck. And He was not wearing a pink band, just as Zolahart wore a black one, He flashed a yellow one. I don't know what's so colourful about good bands. I thought this band is supposedly a very strong one, full of magics that only he can do. Let me tell you these coloured bands tempt me. I really need one.'

'Go and colour your band then.' Justin said. 'What happened next?'

'After a few moments we were so confirmed that he was actually the God; that we never ever tried to ask him for any proof.'

'Never asked?' Romella said. 'Then may be he's not real?'

'No.' David said. 'He is.'

'But why did He meet you?' Justin said. 'Who-are-you?'

'He did have some reasons.' David said. 'But even I am not much satisfied with those.'

'Like what?' Romella asked.

'He said that I was the only spirit who was born just when one cycle of this universe had been completed. That is, I was born exactly one cycle after his birth.'

'And how many cycles are there?' Justin asked.

'You asked that like you've understood what a cycle means.' David said. And Justin gulped and looked at Romella.

'Well,' David said 'we didn't ask him about it right then because right then it did not appeal to us at all. We were standing in front of Him. And we were behaving very devotedly . . . like very decent pupils. He said Semester was also different but the reason should not be told because everyone will come to know about it when it happens. Ya, that meant that he could see the future. He said he could do it ever since he was aged seventeen.' David shut Justin's awestruck mouth with his hands.

'Man; how didn't anyone yet come to know he's alive?' Justin said.

'That's a good question but the answer is, he said spirits have tried to be strong and powerful, and no one knows that it was Him who had tackled with them, no one gets a hint how things abate. Remember the famous Klary incident? And the Salt attacks? They both were handled by him.'

'Man . . .' Justin said with twinkling eyes. 'What a hero . . . I just found I never read much about him.'

Romella said, 'This is so difficult to digest.'

'Shut up.' David said. (that was enough to shut her up for the next hour) 'So where was I . . .'

'Salt attacks.' Justin shot back.

'Ya. So you know what? Paradis told me a famous personality was soon going to rock the system. But God knows how much his soon means. I mean he's lived for so long that it won't be a wonder if three lives like ours put together mean a nap for him. Though, as I told you, fifty blays later me and Sim dropped in front of Zolahart and he had rocked the universe.'

'How did he look like?' Romella made a sudden question.

'He was looking . . . really so . . . different from us though He was basically quite the same. He had such a captivating and divine impression. He was full of light and . . . Godliness . . . He was super duper natural.'

'So but what did he say before he left? And why did he meet you then?'

'He said he had come to make us believe in good. He also said he had pretty few people have known about him being alive. Right then other than Semester and me, one more spirit knew that. And then we felt a bit more normal. At last he reminded us not to discuss it anyhow. And like I told you he was working on how to not feel idle and alone, he had found the solution. He said if he could be alive when required, and if he could end himself when he wished, the problem would be solved. He said that he had inferred one thing from this; there are just two things that are final. Can you guess what they are?'

'Are you making that dialog to us?' Justin said cautiously.

'Oh well, yeah.' David said. 'Sir Paradis asked us this actually. We couldn't even guess at first. Then Semester said, foolishly, birth is not final. And Paradis laughed and said my child, I didn't ask you what is least absolute. Birth is not absolute, instead it is the best example for a thing which can be said to come to an end even before it has happened. The final things are end and eternity. When I become alive or end myself as and when I wish, both of these final things no more remain the final. Goodbye. And, he went . . . along with his yellow shield. And his yellow band . . .'

'So?' Justin said. 'Does the issue of these final things have any relevance to us, or you?'

'That's exactly what Sim and me had wondered. But we haven't been able to figure it out.'

'Well . . . Was that the first and the last time you met him?' Justin questioned.

'Ya.' David gave a short reply.

'What?' Justin said, looking disturbed. 'So? You mean telling stories will help Sim?'

Romella kept looking at their faces. David didn't seem answerable. But after sometime he said, 'Paradis had told me that two people who knew his reality could talk to him if they tried together.'

'Then why did you need three?' Justin said, trying to say that he deserved a special corner in this outstanding story. 'Romella also finds it hard to digest.'

'I don't.' Romella argued like a kid.

Justin ignored and said 'So but I think Paradis is not our personal servant and if the matter had been widely important, he would have already helped Sim.'

'We can talk to Him.' David said.

'You'll trouble Him for your friend?' Justin said, standing up angrily.

David found this reaction rebelling and he stood up and shouted 'Sim is important to Paradis as well. That is why he said he met her and me. Otherwise it could have been a bookworm like you.'

'Just shut up.' Justin said and left.

'Don't stop him.' David said to Romella just as she was going to open her mouth after so long. 'He can't go. The house is shielded by me, you know that.'

'Hope so he doesn't know how to break it?' Romella asked.

'Oh he doesn't. He's not an official' David said as he settled on his seat. 'He's just a bookworm.'

'Shut up.' Justin said, part of his head visible from the edge of the door. 'That's how you talk about me. Rubbish.'

'Get back Justin.' Romella told Justin.

'Have to.' Justin said, coming to his place.

'I had to tell you both. You both are my friends and you both were equally worried for Sim.' David pacified.

'It's not right to talk to Him just because Sim is in danger!' Justin said. 'I am amazed that you still decided to do this after thinking for so long.'

'I told you even Paradis cares for Sim.' David said. 'She is not an ordinary girl. And even if she was, it's far better for Paradis to rescue her than to get bored. After all, what else is he alive for?'

'Don't call Him by His name.' Justin pointed out.

'Paradis is not a name. It's a designation now.' David said. 'You'll keep blabbering Sir Paradis Sir Paradis Sir Sir Sir all the time?'

Romella was the audience.

'Now come on, let's talk to Paradis.' David said.

'All right.' Justin sighed. 'You ready, Romi?'

'Ya. No. I mean we should think what to say and how, no?'

'What's there to think?' David said with pride. 'We want Semester and even Paradis must be knowing she's missing. He may even know where she is or what happened to her.'

'Right.' Romella didn't argue. 'What do we say to contact him?'

'There's nothing different.' David said 'Just do it the way you've always been doing it.'

'I need to spend a very little time with myself.' Justin said, getting up. 'Don't be mistaken. But I'll just be back from the washroom.'

'He's over reacting.' David muttered.

'Over acting.' Romella corrected.

CHAPTER 6

THE CHANGE OF COURSE

Semester's house had been sealed. The investigation department believed it had undertaken some useless items like her personal diary which was not regularly updated (and was mostly written in a code-language), a magic box that was named 'My major adventures, (except the final things)', a prism and a printer with 'Prohibited Plaryzomes Lab Instrument' engraved on them, and an old-withered gold frame.

However, the matter remained unresolved and it was a common belief in the public that it'd make its place as a black chapter in the history. Semester's parents had spent three blays almost in offices. When no milestone had been made in investigations, they insisted Semester's friends be inquired for clues.

They were resting in an empty cabin. Rose was still disturbed and her rosy cheeks were looking dry. Peter, a man with a medium built was very practical. As he had always done, he was doing his work sincerely and it was unpredictable how tensed he was. However, Rodge, Semester's younger and a hundred one percent restless brother was still at Plaryzomes, but whenever he called up, he was mostly handled by Rose. Sometimes, Peter didn't have much patience to answer his worries.

Rose was just hoping that some progress would be reported when the local official passed by, followed by three junior officials.

'This should not go to the infolet department.' She was saying as he walked. 'It'd be a blunder.'

'Yes Madame.' One of the junior officials said.

'The case is now getting impossible.' The official said before entering the other room.

'What happened?' Rose asked Peter.

'I will just check.' Peter said.

'The official was saying the matter is getting impossible.' Rose added.

'They must be talking about some other matter.'

'We can not be sure.' Rose said.

Just then, a junior official came up to them and said, 'I'm sorry to disturb you. Mam has asked you to meet her in her cabin.'

'I told you.' Rose said, getting up in a hurry.

Peter stood up the junior official lead them to the Local Officer.

'Mr Peter and Mrs Rose.' The junior official said as they entered the cabin.

'Have your seats. Ahem.' She arranged some documents on her table, and then said. 'We know Sir and Madam, that if we talk about Semester's friends, the best three names we come across are Romella, David and Justin. We also found you had casual conversation with Justin and David. That's fine. You should keep in touch.'

The officer smiled and Peter smiled back. But Rose was still in a hurry. 'That's definitely not what we are here to talk about?' she said.

'Ahem.' The officer continued. 'Well, when you asked us to summon your daughter's friends for help, we . . . quite soon sent them notices to be present here tomorrow. However, during the regular check of the seven spirits who are closest to Semester, we found . . . we just found that all three of them, Justin, David and er, Romella, are shielded to all levels.'

'What are you saying . . .' Peter reacted.

Rose was awestruck as well. 'Oh my god . . .' she whispered.

But the officer continued. 'But they are still in the Atz galaxy. Their last video revealed they were together before they did this thing.'

'What are these kids upto!' Peter lost his patience. 'They won't ever let us be in peace or what? And officer, I bet on it. It must have been David's idea. To shield it all up.'

'Mister Peter, please. I understand.' The official said. 'Things are already worse and . . . well, these kids might not be . . . I mean their case is different. They have shielded themselves and it is known they're in the Atz. They were talking about some way of rescuing Semester.'

'Oh me.' Rose said sentimentally.

'Calm down.' Peter said to Rose as he himself cooled.

'Madam, this matter is kind of, very impractical. I'm sorry to say this. I mean after all . . .'

'Mam.' An attendant came to the door and said.

'Yes?' The officer replied, happy to be interrupted in the middle of the discussion.

'Sir the three kids are now in the Ester galaxy.'

'Ahem.' The officer said. 'Er . . . excuse me.' She stood up and went outside, whispering something to the attendant about behaving wisely.

As and when David and the rest two had together tried to contact Paradis, they found themselves in the Quixie flier. However, it was a very unusual experience. The flier was not as quick as it was supposed to be and it was probably a dummy.

'I thought we were just trying to contact.' Justin said as the slow Quixie flier engulfed them.

No matter how slow, it took them to a strange place. It was dark all around. Lots of twinkling stars were visible, but they were very distant.

'Where are we?' Romella's voice came from in between David and Justin.

'What are you doing here Romi?' David said, pulling her out from between them. 'Relax. We are shielded.'

'Don't chat.' Justin said. 'My mom n dad would be damn worried.'

'So?' David said. 'You think my mom and dad are giving a party, right?'

'No no no n na nooh.' Romella said. 'Don't. Don't please start here. Now it's all looking silly. Where's the God?'

'I don't know . . .' David muttered. 'He should be here.'

'What dyoo mean he's here. Is it hide and seek?' Justin said.

David thrust his palm on Justin's face and said 'Quiet.'

'Was it the same when you and Sim were about to meet Paradis?' Romella asked.

'Don't think so.' David said.

'This is so stupid.' Justin muttered. 'It is.' He said loudly as David gave him a look.

After looking here and there in the hope that something happens, David was curious to regain his image. 'I guess just two of us should try at a time. Paradis said two basically, I guess. That's the way.'

'Again?' Justin asked.

'Ya.' David said. 'Who's coming? I think you, Justin?'

'Ya. You stay back, Romi. Or rather what'd you do here? Get back to David's place right?'

Romella wanted to convey she shouldn't be treated as a surplus, but she just nodded her head as a sign of okay.

'Look, Romi. We really wanted you to come but . . . now we have no choice. We need your help that's why we all are here together. But, let's give it a try and I hope you don't mind.'

'Ya.' Romella agreed to the decision that was not hers. She basically wanted the task to be done.

'All right. Contact Paradis.' David and Justin said together. They opened their eyes just to find no change.

'Is it that only those whom Paradis has met can contact him?' David asked.

'Are you mad!' Justin said. 'We are sure of practically nothing and yet we are shielded to all levels for a stupid adventure.'

Romella had understood by now that they had failed to contact Paradis.

'Let's get back to your home first of all.' Justin said.

But now, they couldn't even do that.

'Oh no.' Justin said.

'We can't go back . . .' Romella said, ready to cry.

'I've no idea.' David said. 'But yes, before we met Paradis, I told you we couldn't get out of the nebula or go anywhere on our own. The same is happening now.'

'What a similarity.' Justin clapped. 'Hey, why don't you try to go to where you first met Him? Though I know we are not getting the hell out of here at all.'

'No he's not there now.' David said, trying to think of something else.

'Oh really. Did he mail you?' Justin asked, looking frustrated. 'Enough. Give the rest two of us the chance to decide now, right Romi?' Justin said, overtaking the scene.

'Huh? Eh . . . ya.' Romella replied.

'And me and Romi have decided,' Justin said, 'that your role is over.'

David stared at Justin and sighed.

The three felt totally insecure and specially David, who was prone to be blamed for this.

After some targeting conversations, the three finally sat down on the invisible floor.

David shut his eyes and randomly murmured words to find a solution. Unintentionally, he said, 'Ninety degree extreme to the direction the lights . . . er . . . Take me where I met Paradis. Huh. Take to . . .'

'Hey!' David opened his eyes. Romella and Justin also turned spontaneously.

The slow Quixie flier of Paradis had again appeared, but only around David.

'How did you do that?' Justin shouted.

'Just say ninety degree to where that . . . er . . . no . . . where I . . . (swoosh)' David had disappeared.

Romella and Justin exchange dumb looks.

'What next?' Romella exclaimed.

'Ninety degree to where . . . er . . . that' Justin said. He sat down again, shut his eyes and said, 'Ninety degree to . . . Take us to David. Take us ninety degree to the nebula which David mentioned. Ninety degree . . .'

David reached the place where he had met Paradis two slouts ago. He couldn't find anything familiar though. It looked like just another part of the universe, but it was the extreme part. It lied next to where the universe ended and as David could not see anything beyond the end of the universe. The end of the universe was neither dark nor sufficiently bright. It could not at all be seen. It was nothing in fact. It was precisely blank, in all aspects and without any comparison with the blank things we usually come across.

By the time David had clearly come out of the Quixie flier, he discovered that on the other side of him, there was much else.

He fell back when he saw around a dozen spirits near him, who could not see him.

'There's nothing here.' David thought. He whispered, 'Take me back to Justin and Romella.' But nothing happened. 'What the heck. Why can't I go where I want in this stupid slow flier. And anyway, why can't I use the normal flier.' He thought. 'I'm shielded thank god . . . well thank god? But thanks for what . . . Where is Paradis. And what are these morons doing here. At the exact spot.'

He held his head high and straightened his spine very comfortably. 'Adventure.' He murmured stylishly and paced closer to the group of men and women.

'It is not a very strong clue maybe, but maybe it is.' A very short man, or rather dwarf man said. He was holding something.

A woman with long bushy hair emerged from the group behind him. 'Yea.' She said. 'But Sir there is virtually nothing over here so we can seal this place now and leave. Though I doubt anyone ever comes here.'

'Wait for sometime till we study this place.' Another said.

David came closer to them. He was still wondering what they were upto. 'They know Paradis? Oh nope. They're so confused.' He thought. And then he said out loudly. 'You are confused.' He experienced how it felt to be invisibly present. 'Where are Justin and Romi. I knew they can do nothing.'

'Was there a handwriting check? Is it written by Semester?' A lady asked.

'What?' David said.

'Oh no. Not Semester.' The dwarf man replied from near the lady's waist.

'Semester?' David said. Then his eyes fell on what the dwarf man was holding. It was the golden old and withered frame that David immediately recalled was written by Paradis.

'Oh my God.' He said to himself.

'Sir.' A gentleman said now, seated on his knees looking foolishly at the blank end of the universe for clues. 'You know, he only thing that makes me trust the feasibility of coming here is the colour of this dirty and torn frame. Only the colour.'

'And Sir. I know where's the girl.' A bald but young boy said.

'You mean Semester?' Five people replied back as the rest began staring.

'Yes sir.' The boy continued. 'She escaped here. Out of the universe.'

'Who are you?' The dwarf man banged his head before saying. 'Oh, you, Mike.' He sighed. 'I told them. The inductions of non spiritual useless people into the D-staff of our government should be banned. They are the cream of their respective planets! But I'd say, waste out of best.'

'All right seal his area.' The brunette said to three men who were working separately.

'Don't forget to add any point you notice, if you notice.' The dwarf man said. 'We are already running short of landmarks in our investigations.'

'Officials!' David finally understood. 'Damn and I thought I was helping Sim because the officials could do nothing. And here we are, at the same place. Only that they can fly to wherever they want. Take me to Justin. Huh. Useless.'

'Sir may I include this point,' Mike asked, smiling ear to ear. 'There is actually a place like what is mentioned in the golden frame.'

'No!' the dwarf man said, and the impact of Mike's huge smile being lost was profound on his face.

'Let's go.' The dwarf official said after some time and soon all of them assembled.

'All of us to the office.' Mike said just before the dwarf boss opened his mouth.

The Quixie flier surrounded the group and David stayed put, his eyes on the frame. But contrary to what David expected, the Quixie flier took him along and he lost his balance due to the sudden force. His shield hit the little officer.

'What? Was that you Mike? You want to get fired?' The official said, looking tormented.

David quickly stepped away.

'Me Sir? But I didn't do anything.'

With this they reached an office. David didn't notice where the dwarf officer went. The group dispersed to do their respective work.

'A local office.' David said. 'Still, it should've been shielded. To be fair, I shouldn't have been able to enter. I'm an outsider. Anyway, will complaint about it some other time.' He followed Mike to the third cabin. Two others also accompanied.

A very old man was sitting was sitting idle there.

'Oh yes. Let me see what you've got.' He said.

Mike and the other two handed over the observations to him.

The old man went through them roughly. Well actually none of them had more than five lines, other than Mike's.

'Is this what we are going to present in the Outer Senate's meeting tomorrow?' the old man said.

'You're boring me.' David said and came out. 'Take me to Justin.' He tried again. 'No? All right then, okay you can take me to Romella. Take me to Semester then! Okay then how could you take me to the extreme north when I was far better with my friends! Hang on. That slowy flier of Paradis didn't take me anywhere but it did carry me out there. Where I met these officials who could get me here to this office. There may be a reason for this.'

'Sir.' A familiar sound reached David.

He looked around. 'Dad! What are you doing here!'

'Sir!' His dad went to the dwarf officer. 'My son, is there any news of him?'

'Yes.' The dwarf man said. 'There's news. He was in no galaxy around moments before. In no galaxy, clearly. I don't mean we couldn't find which galaxy he was in. He was not missing; just somewhere in the empty lonely spaces. And though his house is probably soon going to be unshielded by us. Yes.'

'That's all?' His dad asked.

'No. There's more. Have a seat Mister Jonas. Ya now your son is now in this Atz galaxy back again, but his friends are still in the Ester. Adding up to the mess, completely.'

'And sir?' Jonas asked.

'And? Where's your daughter Mister Jonas?'

'In Plaryzomes sir, why?'

'So and you take care she remains there. I'm sure they've taught her by now how to shield herself up, to all levels. Rest all we are trying.'

'All right.' Jonas stood up looking upset and unsatisfied.

As Jonas got ready to use the Quixie flier back home, David jumped to stand next to him. But only Jonas got carried away.

'What's going on!' David said. 'What am I gonna do now? I can't even pull myself back from this situation.'

David noticed things getting yellow. He doubted Paradis would come there. Then he saw a watery image of Paradis in front of him.

'Lord, you here?' He said.

'It's just that you are watching me.' Paradis said very calmly. The warmth in his voice immediately made David forget all his worries.

'Why couldn't I talk to you with my friends? Er . . .' David raised the question. Paradis smiled. David hesitated to proceed, but continued somehow. 'Em sorry. I couldn't keep the secret. I knew I was helping Semester, who is outstanding in your opinion. I had an intuition it was not a small problem I'm bothering you for.'

'I knew you would go against your words even while you were making the promise to keep my secret.'

'You . . . Oh, the future foreseeing thing.' David said. 'Now I'm not guilty at all.'

He was well absorbed in the light of Paradis and the world around had disappeared for him.

Paradis continued. 'I have this responsibility to interfere when there's no other option. But it will make nature artificial, and my magic unethical. Also, I never underestimate the powers of others. I don't wish to be helpful every time, either.'

A man of the office walked straight near David and hit his shield.

'Something's here!' He shouted.

David looked at Paradis worriedly. A few officials and appointments came to the man and asked him what had hit him.

'Yes, I could have stopped that from happening. And so I could have stopped Semester's kidnap.'

'She's kidnapped?' David shockingly asked.

'There's a shield over here!' A woman came hurriedly. 'He had hit a shield! Quickly, we are to break it.'

'Indeed, in simple word.' Paradis continued talking to David, seemingly unmoved. 'Now let me take you away. To where I live.'

David didn't question. The slowy flier, as he called it, appeared around them. Even in the flier, Paradis floated a level above David. They landed near a huge house. It could have any number of rooms between five hundred to a thousand. Innumerable angels were moving in the corridors, some playing violin. A few were carrying heavenly cuisines. The place had strong positive vibes and even the non living things seemed blissful.

Everything was built with intricacy and beauty. David felt being the odd one out. His feet were coveting to run into.

'You may get only this close.' Paradis read him.

'Do you add something new to it all the time sir?' David asked, trying to sound like he had never thought of getting any closer either.

He turned around when he didn't get an answer. But Paradis was nowhere to be seen.

David started feeling as if something is going to not to let him be a spirit. Everything got blurred. He felt every bit of him getting coagulated and that eventually it would fall out. He just knew something pallid was appearing next to him but he was busy fighting for his spirit. Everything was faded for him at the moment. At the end, he felt like being as enlightened as a small star. And he was actually pouring out yellow light. He also found himself tall and grown up. He expected Paradis to be present nearby.

He saw that the figure next to him had cleared up. The light coming out of David was overshadowing the boy's features. David moved away to see clearly who he was and when the effect of his light reduced, he found that the boy was no one, but he, himself.

CHAPTER 7

THE FACE OFF

'This is not real.' David repeated his pet dialog. He had seldom felt so dazzled. He kept on staring at the other David. For once, he wanted to speak but words only reached his epiglottis and got lost.

'Calm down.' The other David said, floating higher than the real David. 'We only exchanged the way we look.'

'Sir? Why?' David gasped.

'You are only looking like me, and I am only looking as if I were you.' Paradis said, not paying heed to David's query.

'Well. I had got worried.' David said, looking instantly relieved. 'But till when?'

Like most of the times, answering David did not appeal to Paradis.

'You are required to stay here by the time I unlock your friends, myself and your house.' Paradis said.

'You mean unshield? Why?' David said, as he acknowledged that the yellow band was still with Paradis and not with him. 'I would look perfect with that,' he thought.

'Unlock so that I get kidnapped and your friends get arrested.' Paradis said, only to add to David's confusion.

David opened his mouth for another question but then paused and said, 'alright.'

Paradis didn't make any gesture to that.

'Can I ask one question but?' David said just as Paradis was preparing to do something.

Paradis smiled and David asked him, 'Lord, I don't think I would get nervous while talking to you; or treat you oddly. Because I believe that everyone belongs to you so much that there should be no formality or . . . Nervousness as such. But yet I think giving me your appearance and taking mine, does not regard you.' ('Did I just use the word regard?' David thought)

Paradis shut his eyes, softly held his band and without saying anything at all, vanished.

'Alright.' David muttered.

Paradis entered David's house, without requiring to break the shield around it. In the long run, these normal pink band shields never were a big deal for Him.

Joz and the rest of Zolahart's enemies were still there. They had by now acknowledged that a shield was present at the spot and had to be dismantled.

Just then, the officials arrived near the back door for the same purpose.

'What the hell.' Joz muttered. 'Don't worry! They can't see us.'

'Mark it here.' An official said. 'Clarify it. I don't have all the time.'

'We don't have to be noticed at all.' Joz announced. 'Let them break the shield for us now. We will only check in for David. But I don't want the officials to get any inkling of our presence!'

Paradis could see everything and every one, including the shielded army of Zolahart. He smiled and floated up to the front door where Joz and his team stood.

The officials, facing the back side of the house were preparing for the task's execution.

Paradis shut his eyes, held his wrist where he wore the yellow band and said, 'Unlock Romella 12 and Justin 13 present together eighty five miles from Moc de Ester. Unlock this house and then me.'

Slowly, David's house came into the picture. A few noticed from the very beginning while the rest just followed.

'Had I ordered yet?' The officer shouted at his juniors. 'Who did this?'

Paradis, now unshielded, pulled his yellow band to his elbow to hide it. He examined the two pink bands he was holding, wore one of them, and kept the other one safely under his collars. He deliberately stepped out of the front door. Zolahart's army had already run towards the door and spotted him as soon as he stepped out.

'Take that!' Joz ordered.

Almost all the men covered the door area and two of them grabbed whom they thought was David.

'. . . . this kind of indiscipline. Now get inside!' The officer's voice came from the other side of the house.

'Bravo. Get out of here. Location two. Quick!' Joz said.

With that, all of them got into the Quixie Flier, on their way to get David's memory washed.

At the same time, Romella and Justin were sitting uselessly where David had left them.

They had been sitting silently and Justin was feeling sleepy. He was sitting with his head lying over his hands. Romella was entertaining herself with the jerks Justin's head suffered every time he dozed off.

Feeling uncomfortable, Justin held up his head but his eyes were half shut. He saw someone coming. He opened his eyes and tried to focus.

'Romi, is that an angel?' He said.

'Must be.' Romella replied. 'So late. Yet good for us.'

As it came closer, they found it was not an angel. It was a little boy, with no light, and a dull and odd face. His eyes looked down and his skin was uneven and not lively.

'A beggar!' Justin exclaimed.

'Shut up Justin. Mind your language. Soul is the word.' Romella squeaked.

'Thank god we are shielded.' Justin sighed, feeling sleepy again.

But the boy came up to them, standing in front of Justin, and said 'Please.'

'I didn't know the souls can't do any magic but can see right through the shields.' Justin wondered.

'I can't see through shields mister.' The boy said.

'You can't?' Justin confusedly said, 'but I thought I'm shielded.

'Sir please. I need one room to stay.' The boy said.

'ONE ROOM TO STAY! Get-away! Some generous fools give you ice to cool yourself and that's more than enough. How dare you!'

Romella too didn't stop Justin this time.

'But it's not my fault that unlike you I'm the spirit of a planet, and not a star.' The boy justified himself.

Souls were the non magical, or so called non-spiritual beings, who had been in existence as early as the spirits had. Similar figurine, only duller and weaker looking body that was very warm, and frequently needed ice to cool down. However, the distressing part of their being was the fact that for a spirit, regular contact with the souls would lead to gradual, unnoticeable absorption of their magical energy by the non-magical aura of the souls. Hence, though unintentionally, a line was drawn between the souls and the spirits. Although not falling under bigotry or prejudice, it continued to exist and made souls feel inferior. In the world of pure righteousness, while evil spirits like Zolahart taught the difference between the good and the bad, the discrimination against souls, though due to understood reasons, was a dark spot in the stainless spirituality.

'Spirit-of-a-planet? Call it soul! That's the word for you. How dare you use the word spirit! I'll screw you, wait, er, wait until I can. I'll get you arrested.'

'You are under arrest.' A dominant voice came from behind them. Two local officers stood there.

'There's actually no shield!' Justin muttered to Romella, who nearly shivered.

'Don't move.' The officer said.

'He called himself a spirit.' Justin complained, pointing at the boy. 'And he bothered me for getting a room. Can you believe it?' Justin said, preparing to escape.

'Stop there.' The officer held Justin's hand, who in turn was holding Romella's.

'Back to the office' the officers said, 'of Moc de Ester.'

In location two, the David-looking Paradis was searched for his band. Not at all compromising with his respect, Paradis was floating a little above the rest, but no one noticed. No one bothered about it for the time being. His pink band was removed and confiscated. The searching stopped there, the other pink band under his collar and the yellow band remained intact. He was tackled by five men so that he couldn't move, though he was already not trying to rebel.

'The master says he will come here.' Joz said. 'Get the boy to that cell and let him wait.'

The five men escorted Paradis inside. Joz rubbed his hands and murmured, 'And having done two inaugurating works, I will now become one of his most beloved hands.'

Paradis had been very humble to face all this. Without resisting, he moved with the five men to the chamber. Like for us, Jesus let himself be crucified, like Mohammad let go of his beloved son, like Rama abandoned his luxury and later his wife. All such instances only make Gods greater.

Pushed inside the door, Paradis was left to wait for Zolahart and the door was shut behind him.

When Paradis was alone, he looked at the dirty green walls of the room. He had not been able to quite read them for the last two slouts.

'So all over here are signs of evil.' He said to himself.

He patiently waited for Zolahart to arrive. He slid his hand under his sleeves and pulled his yellow band back to its right place.

Finally, some activity occurred at the door. Sounded as if there were more than one.

Slowly, the door opened. Zolahart entered, as always, floating above his attendants. He had a collection of rage and victory in his eyes, as seldom seen before. His hair was messy and his spirituality was visibly dominant by the devil inside him. His greenish skin made him look different.

He raised one of his hands up to his shoulder level and the attendants shut the door.

Paradis looked directly into his eyes calmly. He was floating above Zolahart's level.

Zolahart's expressions changed sharply when he noticed this and he immediately rose up.

Paradis didn't move for a few moments and then again rose up to float above Zolahart's level.

'How dare you!' Zolahart roared, his eyes turning black with fury. He pulled his sleeve and held his black band.

Paradis smiled, and without delaying, pulled his sleeve and flashed his yellow band.

Zolahart's eyes felt a weird irritation on spotting it. He avoided it and growled, 'Whatever that is, you are as nothing as that girl was.' He rose above Paradis again and said. 'I don't ge a damn.'

Paradis ignored this completely and rose up again until his head was just about to touch the ceiling. 'I won't let that colour touch me.'

Flabbergasted, Zolahart extended his hands and gathered power to slowly create a green light by pulling his hands together. Meanwhile, Paradis also collected his energy and gathered yellow light. Zolahart threw the green light towards Paradis, who threw back the yellow. Both the lights ran towards each other. In a matter of fractions of a second, they rammed and with a blast, the complete hall rocked. The room was bursting with a mixture of both the lights. As the intensity decreased, both the men saw that the green light had finished while the yellow one had reduced to a twinkle and died out with a pop.

'I had not expected this.' Paradis said, looking worried.

Nearly all visible veins on Zolahart's face puffed and his face had awful angry expressions. He moved his hand all around himself and threw green light on Paradis. Paradis quickly diverted it towards the sidewall and the room rocked heavily. A huge part of the side wall broke off.

Zolahart roared angrily and rose up, his head touching the ceiling. He shouted, 'You think you can battle me. You won't even live for long now.'

'I had never been able to read your shields well enough and easily; until now.' Paradis calmly said.

Outside the hall, Zolahart's women and men were wondering what all the noise might have done to David. But Joz ordered no one would try to interfere.

'This pink band is fake.' A woman reported to Joz.

'What?' Joz said, snatching the pink band that was undertaken from Paradis.

Inside, the fight had come to a small halt.

'You are not him.' Zolahart thoughtfully said.

'I am not whom?' Paradis replied.

'That boy.'

'Definitely.' Paradis gave a true and short reply.

'No one can stand against me in any way.' Zolahart yelled. 'No one can give a try. I have the magics no one has ever seen or even thought of doing.'

'I have changed my appearance.' Paradis said. 'Have you ever seen or thought of doing it?'

Zolahart's chest was visibly moving in and out as he breathed heavily with anger.

'I-am-the-master.' Paradis articulated in a slow manner.

'I won't see you until that bloody pride in your eyes is lost! I don't even need to handle you myself. My liitle ones are enough for this purpose. I saw you captivated in all your senses. I saw the fear in your eyes and now I must get to some other job. Soldiers!' Zolahart roared, he jerked his hand and the door fell open. 'Break his hands!'

The soldiers standing outside, already confused, ran in and were shocked to see the scenario.

To them, David looked as calm as they had brought him in, and Zolahart looked offended. Adjusting themselves to the shocking circumstance and taking Paradis lightly, they were just preparing to obey when Paradis swiftly moved his hands around and threw a scattered yellow light towards all the soldiers. The yellow light swept all of them off and Paradis flew out of the cleared doorway.

He held his yellow band and aimed at Joz, who proficiently threw pink light at Paradis. Very easily, Paradis diverted it towards Zolahart just to distract him shortly. Zolahart floated forward, finished off the light and came out, only to see Paradis vanish, taking Joz along.

CHAPTER 8

JOZ'S LABORIOUS TRANSITION

Joz was taken by the David-looking Paradis to a ruined palace dating from ancient times. Some souls had occupied the place. They could be seen moving through the broken corridors, weak and dull men and women, girls and boys. Some of them were fighting for a piece of ice that one of them had managed to get. In a corner, a soul, a boy it was, was lying down, warm and emergently needing ice, but no one took notice, or rather no one could stake one's own life for his.

Joz made a hateful expression about the site.

'Leave this place until I'm here.' Paradis said, creating big blocks of ice using his yellow band and floating them towards the souls. In an undisciplined way, all the souls jumped on the ice pieces and then obeyed Paradis to disappear. It was similar to a stampede site. One of them finally had the goodwill of throwing one ice block towards the dying soul.

'How did you escape the master?' Joz asked Paradis, now surprised at his behaviour and skills.

The souls were still disappearing with pops.

'And you talk like that to these useless creatures.' Joz added.

Paradis fashioned a yellow shield around Joz and said. 'It'll be me who questions and you who answers.'

Joz, trying to break the shield, said, 'You think you'll live for long now?'

'You think you can break this shield even though all your army put together could not break a simple one around David's house?'

Joz stopped abruptly and said, 'You mean your house.'

'Oh yes.' Paradis said. 'I must tell you I don't fancy, at all, hurting creatures. So, please tell me where Semester is and how to reach there.'

Joz started laughing at this. 'You're scary!' Then he quietened and said. 'Though I don't believe you were in front of my master moments ago, at the threshold of getting your memory tempered with, and right now you are trying to torture me, yet I don't think you are here for long. It must have been Master's plan to let you go away. Must be a reason behind it.' Joz got thoughtful.

Paradis shut his eyes and whispered to himself. 'I feel sorry. But this is what has to happen for the ultimate good. I know, also, I will take care of him, as and howsoever time tells me to.'

Joz tried to listen, getting not more than half a dozen words arbitrarily. Without any warning, Paradis banged Joz's head onto the shield around him.

Joz forgot where he was. He situated it to the incident when Zolahart had hit a man in the meeting.

He opened his eyes and took control of himself. He heard Paradis say, 'I don't intend to do this. I can free you of all evil and chains. Only tell me what I asked.'

'You're the weirdest boy of your age.' Joz said, with considerably changed expressions and tone.

'That was not an appropriate answer.' Paradis responded.

'Nor will it be.' Joz said, frightened. He held his band and created another shield inside the one made by Paradis.

Paradis waited and then held his yellow band. He muttered something and Joz's shield broke down at once.

Joz couldn't believe it. His eyes had opened up to the danger level and his upper and lower eyelashes touched his forehead and face respectively.

He speedily said, 'Talk to my master.' But definitely, it was useless to give a try. 'Talk to master.' Joz repeated.

Paradis let Joz to try to his satisfaction.

'I'll take my leave of you while you keep trying.' Paradis said and vanished.

Joz was utterly confused by now. He thought David had gone insane. But as soon as Paradis left, he began trying with redoubled efforts, thinking that it must have been Zolahart whose attack had made David go mad.

Paradis headed straight to where the scenic beauty of his household still held David mesmerised, though David was unable to get closer to the palace. Twice he tried to get nearer and both the times he got shocked away by invisible premises. He also tried to talk to the angels about the palace, about the unrevealed facts of that world, or to just have the master feeling, but no one entertained him. Everyone there knew the difference between the God and someone else with his appearance. At most, the angels smiled at him, and all David knew was that it was Paradise where Paradis lived.

'David.' He heard Paradis call him.

'Yes sir.' He ran towards Paradis, who was standing next to an extremely handsome angel. While running, he thought he would fall in love with the angel if he himself were a girl. For sure.

'Er, yes.' David said, talking to Paradis, but staring at the angel. Now, he could smell a sweet fragrance. He felt lovely and smiled.

Paradis made a one sided introduction. 'Cupid, this is David.'

David's jaw dropped loose.

'My purpose of going to Zolahart was to read his locations and to give him a hint him of my existence.' Paradis said and took out the pink band from under his collars and handed it over to David.

'Zolahart—is—alive!' David bellowed, 'Oh my God! It's him!'

'This might help Semester.' Paradis told David. 'Joz is a key person who kidnapped her. He has been detained by me. Now the rest is your job. Only remember; just as poison kills poison, evil counters evil.'

'And love makes hatred uncomfortable.' Cupid said.

'Very true.' Paradis said. 'That is why Cupid will effectively help you in deflecting Joz from his dark thoughts.'

Paradis shut his eyes and David again felt his body undergo renovation. He stopped looking at Cupid and shut his eyes. His skin felt like sticking together. He knew this time what was going on. He patiently waited for it to get over. His fists were tightly closed. Ultimately, he shrunk back to being himself. He looked at himself, at Paradis and then again at Cupid.

'David, your magic will be able to penetrate my shield around Joz. Now without delaying, I shall send you both to Joz.' Paradis said.

'Lord, I didn't understand what was the use of giving me your appearance.' David hurriedly said, half sure that he wouldn't be answered. 'You could've simply taken mine. I mean, I didn't make any use of your looks.'

'Exchanging appearances takes less time, is less confusing, and more natural. Moreover, after all, you are the only one ever, with whom I can exchange appearance.'

'What? Wait . . . no wait.' David said. But this time, Paradis sent them for Joz.

Even inside the slowy flier, David was could not keep his eyes off Cupid. He would have been jealous of his looks otherwise, but Cupid was the God of love, and there was no place for negative emotions in his aura.

Soon they reached the sight of the ruins and found Joz desperately trying all ways to set himself free. The tension and unrest on his face normalized when he saw Cupid.

'Sir Joz?' David exclaimed, 'you never looked like a cheat! All this time you faked you were helping us. And, oh my god, you are an awful official!'

'What do you suddenly mean? And whom have you got now?' Joz said. 'How could you get an angel? And . . . What does an angel have to do with us right now?'

'I am Cupid. And I have to do all good with anyone right at anytime.' Cupid smiled.

'That's not ordinary to have him on your side.' Joz thoughtfully said. 'But my powers are strong enough to understand the intensions behind bringing Cupid, if he actually is Cupid. You look good. And I can order my brain not to be overtaken by your sweetness.'

'What would you like to be overtaken by?' Cupid asked.

'Where's Semester?' David said.

'I only like to be overtaken by my master's noble ideas.' Joz replied.

'Would anyone, any one answer me ever?' David said. 'Hey you, take us where she is.'

'Were the ideas noble, if your memory was washed, just as you washed Semester's?' Cupid said.

'WHAT?' David bellowed.

'Or was it noble that you performed your duties you pledged as an official. Was it noble that your house was reached with an army and then you were to be kidnapped like you were going to do to David?'

'WHEN?' David said.

'Or,' Cupid continued, he moved his hand and the place got colourful like a rainbow, fragrant breeze blowing around and yellow dew like blessings of optimism fell on Joz and David 'you would have leaded your life as a faithful and proud official, saving others from discomfort.'

Joz screamed and tried to sway away the dew. 'No!' He yelled. 'You can't do this. I am faithful to my master who gives me power, who must be accompanied by me and others like me to achieve his noble aim! NO!'

Joz covered his head and shut his eyes. He tried to concentrate.

'Let's see what comes out when you gather your energy.' David said, serious about the site.

Joz opened his eyes and yelled, 'Why should I?'

'You wanted to kidnap me? Where's Semester?' David asked.

'No!' Joz said, his devil feeling irritated by goodness.

David also felt like he was being suppressed by Cupid's vibes. He ran away from him and held his own pink band on his wrist. He hit Joz hard with a pink rod that he thus created and Joz's nose began to bleed.

Joz moaned and wiped the blue blood away.

'We love you.' Cupid said. 'I know you seldom get to hear these words. But we love you, and we want to fill all the interstices of your life with love, just in case you pour out all your mistakes.'

Joz had got dominated by Cupid's positive vibes as soon as David distracted him by hitting him. David threw a beam of pink light towards Joz and gave an electric shock directly to his brains. Joz's head got stuck to the beam and he fell down. He shouted and remembered every pain he had given others, every sin he had committed, every evil he had chosen, he powered his hands and created a green light that grew bigger as he poured more of his evil into it. He held his pink band and breathed Cupid's breeze, and thought good. He remembered all the terrific punishments Zolahart meted out to his own men and women and, then he feared them,—disliked them . . . He found the breeze, the cold yellow dews more pleasant than the tensed and evil environment of the locations. He found Cupid's charming face and voice more appealing than Zolahart's bitter and horrific appearances. During this procedure, he purified himself and when he opened his eyes, he found that the ball of green light, that contained his dark character, was half his size.

David held his band impulsively and directed his hand towards the green ball. The green ball rose up and David took control of it.

'Where's Semester?' He asked loudly.

'Let me take you there.' Joz said, now looking more spiritual and normal. 'Wait, but you've shielded me.'

'Oh . . . have . . . I?' David said in a deteriorating volume.

'What do you mean?' Joz said, Cupid's dew still falling on him.

'Oh . . .' David said, 'What next?' He said, looking at Cupid, maintaining control of the ball of light.

'Next, Joz will lead a normal life. With pride.' Cupid said.

'Oh not that!' David said.

'Next? Next you break this shield!' Joz said.

Just then, the watery image of Paradis reappeared. David was taken aback for a moment when he noticed it, but didn't let the other two have cognizance of it. It seemed that only David could see the translucent Paradis.

'Pretend to unlock the shield.' Paradis said.

Sighting Joz's confused face, David held his band and punched in the direction of Joz. Paradis simultaneously shut his eyes and unlocked the shield.

'Take David and me to Location three.' Joz said, without thinking of making use of the opportunity.

David quickly saw the calm face of Paradis and the lovable one of Cupid get replaced by the sky blue walls of the Quixie flier, the normal Quixie flier. He kept control of the green light Joz had created and held it along behind him.

Inside the flier, David saw Joz expressions change. Without Cupid, Joz was tempted again to take in the green light. The fear of Zolahart also threatened him to stop David from reaching Semester. He too a dive at David who then lost control of the ball. The ball fell down on the flier's running floor and lagged behind.

Both David and Joz ran against the Quixie flier but the flier was much quicker. Both of them magically targeted the ball but Joz targeted better and drew the ball towards himself. David blocked the way by creating a pink web. The ball hit hard on it and broke into two. David immediately threw the bigger half forwards and Joz found it more promising to take on the other part in the meantime. He was at the verge of getting it but David jumped on him. The green chunk nearly touched David, but he saved himself by twisting his hand and fractured his wrist. Not giving up, he managed using the other hand and threw the smaller piece away. The piece ran behind to remain lost forever.

Joz threw David away and he hit the wall of the flier. The wall chafed David's head and he fell down. By the time he revived he saw that the larger portion he had thrown forward had approached Joz.

'No!' David shouted, but his broken wrist hindered fast action and Joz directed the piece towards himself with his band.

The green light hit Joz and started pervading into him. Concurrently, they reached Location three.

'Evil counters evil.' David muttered. He held his band tightly and aimed at the light that was getting absorbed into Joz.

Joz was engaged and the sparks were outshining him. David pulled apart some light and threw it towards the shields of the location, which was accompanied by a thunder, alerting the guards.

Without delaying, David gathered as much power as he could, reckoning that it was now or never; he crafted a huge pink fire and hit again.

The shields of the Location broke off.

As one of the guards got ready to construct another shield, Joz hit David but accidentally, David had by now got thrown into the building's premises.

'Thanks.' David muttered as the guard's shield covered the Location, with David already inside it.

One of the guards ran inside while the other attacked David. David rolled over the invisible floor and escaped. He had lost all his energy but he stood up and staggered inside. He saw the other guard standing next to Semester, who looked weak, dumb and fearful.

It was not at all how David had pictured meeting Semester after such a long and difficult time. However, he felt much better and found his power doubled.

He held his band and roped the guard, rendering him harmless, before the guard could reach his band. David ran to Semester where he saw that she was throwing light towards the other guard, who hid his face under his arms to avoid the bright luster. David threw a rod straight to the guard's head and turned around to see the other guard he had just tied up. He was talking to someone with his eyes shut, which definitely mean he was informing others.

David ran towards Semester and gave her the surplus pink band that Paradis had given to him for her. Semester snatched it and looked at David sternly. She felt restless at the possession of the band.

David witnessed she had really lost her memories and said, 'Do you have your memories? Because you just threw out light at that guard . . .'

Semester gave a blank and suspicious expression, and David said, 'We need to get out of here safely.'

He ran to the other guard who was still holding his head and was trying to get up; then David punched him in the gut. Semester rushed out of the room meanwhile and David left the guard and followed her.

There he found Semester satisfying her impatience regarding the band, she was aiming at the already tied up guard and screaming, 'Bounce in the air! Rebound! Hit, hit, hiiiiittt!'

The guard zoomed up in the air and struck back on the invisible ground, and recoiled with the invisible slaps and punches with which he was being treated.

David held Semester's hand and saw that Joz was still overviewing everything from above the location.

'It's been fast but any moment there are going to be hundreds of fighters over here.' David said.

'You have put my life to hardships and pain.' Joz distressfully said.

'Could you help us now, to break the shield around this location?' David hastily said to Zolahart.

'. . . . No.' Joz said.

'Look, Semester, try with me, to break it okay?' David said. At this, he attacked the shield, Semester could not turn up quickly and stammered a dozen haphazard words in all directions.

'No! Look . . . uhh . . .' David said, frustrated.

'Sometimes switching back to being good is the penalty for being bad,' Joz said, holding his band in agreement to helping David.

Not having much time, David recovered himself, and in chorus with Joz, attacked the shield, Semester too shut her eyes and thrust all her anger onto the shield. But the shield did not break.

Suddenly, Joz disappeared. It appeared to David that he had not deliberately gone. Also, the slowy flier appeared round David and Semester.

'I know who did this,' David smiled, 'come on girl, I can't fight any longer with this broken hand.'

CHAPTER 9

SOLEMN GET TOGETHER

Peter and Rose had devoted all their time for Semester. Peter was even ready to accept that he might have lost his daughter enduringly.

Rose was a blend of emotions and strength. She had handled the office work, Rodge, the relatives and herself in a much better way than possible for someone else.

She was writing around the hundredth application, in the office; her Rosy cheeks looking dry, as if all their moisture had made its way through her eyes.

Amidst all this, David and Semester walked in as if they were entering a regular classroom.

'Oh my god!' The officer spotted the duo at once. 'Security!' he screeched.

Rose looked up dully. Her eyes wandered to look out for what was happening, but crowd had promptly screened the sight. Through a very small vacancy, her eyes saw Semester. All this time, Rose had mistaken many girls as Semester, yet she walked straightaway towards the crowd. She struggled to make her way through the cops and she saw David and Semester sitting in the midst.

'Semester!' She stuttered in awe, as tears instantly rolled down her cheeks.

Some office women tried to whisk her away. David got frustrated but he couldn't do much with a dozen of hands ready to wind him.

He shouted to Aunt Rose, 'We're all right.', and then couched as he recalled Semester had lost all her reminiscences.

Rose scarcely heard him. She was still edgy and a worker told her that she would just have to wait until the office was over with its job.

'Just don't let go of these two cartoons.' The officer told.

The cops thrust David and Semester onto a single chair and Semester again got alarmed about her security. Her hand was strictly on her pink band without any exception.

'Careful!' David said, holding his fractured hand.

The information cell was ordered to summon a full-fledged team and David and Semester were taken to the official's cabin.

Jonas, too, arrived and as soon as he did, he said, 'Where's David?' talking to himself because no one else had the time

By this time, the office looked like a store that had offered all its items for free.

"Where . . . Rose . . . !' Jonas worriedly ran towards Rose. 'Madam Rose. Where are the kids?'

Rose was speechlessly gazing at the official's door. Jonas didn't notice the traces of satisfaction on her face. She slowly pointed her hands towards the door.

'Thanks.' Jonas said, on his way to the door.

Only as he had caught a glimpse of Semester, an office man shut the door and said, 'E'm soory sirr. There arre many official proceedings beforre the young couple is sett free.'

'Young couple?' Jonas said, astounded.

'We understand.' Peter's voice came from behind. 'That is definitely important. Thank you.'

'Hello.' Jonas said.

'Hello.' Peter replied, shaking hands.

'Er, Mrs. Rose looked worried. But, Semester looked sound. Everything's all right? Or has David hurt himself or something?'

'Oh as far as they're not missing, they're fine I know.' Peter said. 'I saw him. He looked alright. And Rose's speechlessness . . . that's just some sort of respite. Congratulations.'

'Same to you.' Jonas said, finally relaxing 'Er, excuse me, I'll just call David's mum. She hasn't yet breathed a sigh of relief.'

'I'll inform Rodge too,' Peter said, smiling assuredly.

A secret looking and almost vacant room was where David and Semester were taken under strict supervision.

David's fractured hand was temporarily fixed, and he felt no pain.

Now Semester looked totally content. Her face read that everything was over and that it was party time. She readily turned to wherever she was taken.

David's mind could explode any moment, thinking what all the questions he probably would be asked, what all he would answer, and whether he would be able not to mention Paradis and yet or even utter only truth. 'Just a smaaall interview for the two superstars.' The office man with an obnoxious accent said, leading them to a non-empty room this time.

As they entered the enquiry room, David saw two more dear ones jump on sighting him and Semester; Justin and Romella. Like a bicycle without breaks, David marched into the room and straight towards Justin. But an office man held him from the back and redirected him to a table on the other side.

David had entirely forgotten about Justin and Romella. And though he didn't care about it, he had to show that he did.

'Where were you?' he asked using facial expressions.

In response, Justin raised his eyebrows and stared at David, signifying, 'Where do you think we were?'

Romella was constantly gazing at Semester. She kind of said hello to her a couple of times but Semester didn't bother to notice. Already at a great unease, Semester's attitude made Romella feel like a lost and barmy lot. Her face read only one expression, 'I'm involved in a police case.'

Putting aside all this, each of them was predominantly glad that Semester was back. The friends were much better in facing any enquiry or police case now that she was safe.

The enquiry team hovered inside without delay. It appeared to be headed by a very senior official, followed by some officials under him, an investigation team and no one from the news department.

'By the way,' David whispered to Semester, 'you did your indigenous magic on that guard, you threw light at him without your band, if you don't really have memories, how could you?'

Semester looked at Semester and strained her eye brows, 'I don't know what indigenous magic is, but I happened to discover it whle I was alone in Location three.'

'Oh, you rediscovered it,' David said, 'cool, that's why you are my bestie,' he winked.

The senior official took his place and the rest followed. The guilty party also settled down.

'In the presence of honourable Sir Atz, we begin the enquiry.' an official announced.

'I am going to be interrogated by of the head-of-our-galaxy!' David screamed in his mind. Then he stole a look at Semester and imagined how she would panic if she knew how much a Head means.

Justin rearranged his hairstyle and Romella pursed her lips, looking tearful.

'So, where have you been?' Sir Atz began.

Everyone turned to look at Semester; and Semester also turned around.

'Sir is talking to you.' An official said.

'She's lost her memories.' David said, and the room echoed with sounds of all kinds.

For sometime, Justin and Romella looked suspiciously at David, thinking whether it was his latest plan.

Meanwhile, David quickly went through what next to say.

Justin whispered to himself, though deliberately letting Romella listen, 'I knew he just couldn't be that perfect.'

'Silence please. Remain quiet.' An officer said, after he himself quietened down.

'You want to say something, Master David?' Sir Atz said.

David cleared his throat and nodded in a 'yes'.

'Please.' Sir Atz said.

'I set out . . . I mean with Justin and Romella, to look out for Semester. We were really worried and . . . .'

'So were many others. Not to forget her parents.' Sir Atz cut in. 'When the whole universe and the officials were trying to find her, you thought you could do it better, didn't you?'

'Er, yes,' David said, 'and I think I brought her back.'

Sir Atz was taken aback by an answer like that. He blinked a few times, expecting someone from his juniors to stand up for him.

An official said, 'Do you know who you are talking to?'

'Er . . . yes.' David thoughtfully said. 'I'll have to speak the truth. Specially when the Head is questioning me.'

The room was at pin drop silence and Justin was staring at David dangerously.

'How did you find Semester?' Sir Atz asked; and everyone looked at David with grave attention. 'Remember, there will be truth tests for everything you say.'

As confident looking as he was not, David said, 'Sir Atz said that the whole universe and the officials were trying to find Semester, but I'm afraid, the truth is conflicting.'

The room again broke into whispers and gossips but David continued speaking, hoping that it'd get messy and no one would care what he said.

'Joz, an official, was in fact involved in the group that kidnapped Semester. And he came to kidnap me as well. That's how I got to Semester. They were trying to kidnap me and make me lose my memory just like they had made Semester lose hers!"

'There are so many officers named Joz.' The official said.

'Surely.' David said. 'It's more important that even more officials are a part of that criminal group.'

'So you were kidnapped?' An investigation officer asked.

'Er. No. They couldn't find us as we got ourselves shielded.' David replied, and the effect was that the officers felt their patience being tested.

'Then if the question was how you found Semester, why the answer was that you were to be kidnapped?' an official asked.

'Because later Cupid and I went to Joz again, where he had been incarcerated.' David replied.

'Now when did Joz get caught, and who is Cupid?' Sir Atz questioned.

'Sir, Cupid! the God of love!' David said, factually.

'A-truth-test!' Three officials said together.

'And who captivated Joz? You didn't answer.' Sir Atz said.

'A friend of Cupid's. That friend introduced us as well.' David said, feeling the high time.

'What kind of a friend. Certainly not an angel,' an officer said. 'Angels don't involve themselves in any matter that is beyond the scope of love and comfort.'

'Yeah.' David said.

'Yeeaah, now who-was-that friend?' The official continued.

'That friend, oh yeah . . . I was lost, I mean when me, Justin and Romella shielded ourselves, we found that we could no longer use the Quixie flier or contact anyone. But suddenly I tried, and I was taken somewhere. I didn't know where exactly it was and then I heard his voice. He looked ordinary. And he took me somewhere and introduced me to Cupid and said that Joz had been captivated, and now with Cupid's help, I can reach Semester. Yes. This is all absolutely true, I assure you. I mean that friend, I call him a friend because he helped me, that's all. Er, he is like God to me. I hope I get to meet him some other day cause I actually didn't suitably thank him.'

'Very well. It's okay, calm down. We can test that for our assurance. It is not someone ordinary who would captivate Joz and make Cupid help you.' Sir Atz said, with a sarcastic smile.

He raised his hand and signalled the officer not to question David.

'Er, girl. What's your name?' said the official turning to Semester.

'Semester.' Semester replied, as Justin fearfully shot up.

The officer got up and said, 'But he said you remember nothing!'

'Oh no, Joz told me that.' Semester said.

'Alright. How much do you remember?' continued the official. 'Listen. Let me aware you if you have lost your memories: you have a family and there are many people who care for you. But before you get back to them, you ought to take all this seriously. We are officials. So, if you cooperate, we'd be able to find and punish those who . . . troubled you, in so far as Master David's statements are considered true.'

'Officials! Joz and his lot was always afraid of you people. They said the officials might trace us!' Semester found things substantial and vital now. Also, she definitely remembered her sufferings in Location Three. She immediately commenced, 'All right. Ask master David. How he found me and where.'

'Wow. Thanks.' David muttered. 'Er . . .'

'No wait. I want to say something.' Semester cut in.

'Oh right.' An official stood up. 'Explain.'

'Yes I do remember that ever since I opened my eyes I was not a spirit. They had sent me to some different place. Er, Joz and some more wicked spirits, told me they had exiled me to . . . Moc de—Lilac.

But they brought me back and sent me to Location three.' She paused, and said in the way a grandmother tells a ghost story to children, 'And I know more.'

'Silence.' Sir Atz said, 'This is an extremely sophisticated gathering and let it look so. Both shall be sent for truth test now. And Miss Semester's memories shall be granted back to her in case she actually does not possess them. Following which she will answer more dutifully and seriously. David is the most favoured witness. The major questions have been asked. The infolets must be suitably handled about the dispatch of information. Congratulations to every one. The case is dismissed.'

'What?' Some officials and David said.

'But I know more.' Semester said, her voice not audible under the noise of chairs and debates.

Romella looked around as if she had just come alive, Justin got up and Semester waited for David to do something. A few officials told her to follow them for her treatment.

'David stays back.' Sir Atz announced just then.

'Oh, so it's not over.' David muttered to himself in disgust.

'Bye.' Semester said to David.

'Yeah.' David said, forcing a smiling.

Soon, most of the room was vacated. A handful of officials with Atz remained, and he signalled to shut the door.

As soon as the door was shut, the officials started further shielding the room, while sir Atz simply made a table of his hands and placed his head on it. He stared at David with twinkling eyes.

David forced a smile again, a symbol of relaxation.

David felt that the real investigation was to start now. Sir Atz, unlike his status-conscious behaviour, looked more like any other member of the investigation team.

Finally, David visualised that the questions were ready.

As if it was all pre-planned, an official held David's head gently and said, 'It's just a truth test.'

'Shut your eyes, please.' Sir Atz said to David, winking. 'We need to get acquainted with your sub-conscious mind now.'

David blinked and thought he had no role now to play. He shut his eyes slowly. He heard a little movement and then he lost his conscious.

CHAPTER 10

✦
✦ ✦

THE AFTERMATH

'Where—is—Joz?' Zolahart said in a compact voice which was clearly trying hard not to erupt into a roaring grumble.

There persisted sheer silence in the Location two . . . Semester's rescue despite Zolahart's personal involvement, had been obviously insulting, and no one wanted to become the target of Zolahart's anger, for something they had played no role in 'Call him in now.' Zolahart instructed.

A man with Golden cape flowing behind him entered the hall, walked in towards Zolahart alone and stopped in front of Zolahart's huge chair.

'Yes. What is the noticeable piece of information?' Zolahart asked him.

The man seated himself on a front row chair restfully.

'You see Sir; it was actually going to be valuable to have me on your side,' he said, unveiling his other half of the face from under his hair. 'Being the Head of David's and Semester's native galaxy, they escaped from Location three, and straight into my interrogation,' said Sir Atz.

'What—is—the piece of information, Atz?', Zolahart repeated.

'The boy's mind reading concluded that he has never met you,' Sir Atz said. 'David, has never met you.'

Zolahart's eyes winked, he muttered, 'Zolahart is always right. It was not that boy.'

'But it was him who rescued the girl from the Location Three,' Atz added.

Zolahart's eyes shimmered and contracted.

'Lastly, parts of his memories were unreadable,'

A sleek woman with long and ugly front teeth entered from one of the secondary sideways entrances.

She bowed, looking too nervous, and projected David's memories in the room. It was like a small new house gradually appeared inside the hall, with small David, Romella and Justin seated facing each other.

'All right,' David said. 'We are here to talk on what we can do to find Semester. Shield us and this house to all levels.'

The small house of David's transformed into an empty space of the Ester galaxy.

'Wait!' Zolahart said and the ugly-toothed woman shuddered hastily and paused the video.

'He just shielded the house,' Zolahart said, 'he didn't go anywhere.'

'Sir, I told you, parts of the boy's memories were unreadable; remain unknown!' Atz said.

Zolahart breathed in and out in that absence of air, and signalled to continue.

The woman instantly abided by the order.

'Where are we?' Romella said.

'What are you doing here Romi? Relax. We are shielded.' David replied.

'Don't chat. My mom n dad would be damn worried.' Justin said.

'Are we here to watch these child-fights?' Atz interrupted.

'Do not cross your limits Atz!' Zolahart said.

Atz readjusted himself to sit in a more disciplined manner.

'Let me see every nonsense.' Zolahart murmured.

Everyone with severe interest kept watching the confusing video in which scenes unexpectedly and abruptly terminated.

From the helpless sight of the Ester galaxy, the place transformed into the dead end of the Universe, with Romella and Justin no more accompanying David. The officials were present too, with the dwarf officer looking even smaller.

'What is this place?' said Zolahart in undertones, his sharp eyes noticing everything, 'And what is that golden frame that crackpot holds?'

'I only know that it is a very old frame,' Atz said 'very very old, and that it was taken from Semester's house as we can see. Whatever nonsense was written on it was the way to finding this spot.'

David jumped in with the officials and travelled along to their office, where he saw his father.

Zolahart understood much more than he should have, despite nothing being clearly visible; the scenario getting clear in his mind.

'What's going on!' David said, on failing to be carried along with his father, 'What am I gonna do now? I can't even pull myself back from this situation.'

Straight from that point, the scene changed to an eye-opener: Joz was captured, David was standing unharmed, and having on his side—Cupid.

Zolahart kept watching impassively. The funny toothed woman's hand itched, and she was battling hard not to even let it show on her face. No one present in the entire hall dared to do anything save staying put.

'Just one more thing of my interest remains,' Zolahart asked Atz. 'I told you there's much more I want to give to this universe than just my eternity.'

'As the respectable Head,' Atz answered, 'after David' truth test, fixation of his broken wrist and restoration of Semester's memories, I ordered them that they are not supposed to discuss anything about you to anyone, not even to their best of networks or parents.'

'Then I suggest everyone should leave.' Zolahart said. He shut his eyes and teleported away. Huge amounts of suppressed activities followed inside the hall.

There had never been any guard securing Location one, nor had anyone other than Zolahart ever entered the premises as yet. This time, though Zolahart had called upon someone to see him.

Location one, Zolahart's residence was the hugest of all the Locations, the Dark Senate. All green, with embedded greenstones, dirty green smog all around; a horrific site. These rooms were host to the most perilous magic and hard graft of all times.

Bizarre things were lying around, books and frames covering large spaces, frequent lights filling the rooms for short whiles, a silence indigenous to the long lonely story of the walls, samples o experiments resulting in great black magic, aura humming the tales of wisdom that chose a different path, and an untold dark glory that was the home to Zolahart.

'The old golden frame,' Zolahart said to his guest, who was standing in the next room, 'and David's helplessness in travelling on his own, was what I noticed the most.'

'I have no bloody idea of what you are talking about,' the guest said, his dusky magenta body partly in dark due to the presence of one single light at the corner of the room.'

'Satan,' Zolahart said, louder this time, 'Who do you think can Cupid help, at all.'

'Paradis,' Satan, the devil turned angel, the one that fell out of opinion with God, replied, flying into the room from where Zolahart was enquiring him. He landed on one of the wall sides, looking here and there.

'I see.' Zolahart said. 'No more do I feel insulted.'

Satan looked at Zolahart with his narrow eyes, fearlessly and flied towards him, he spiralled around him a couple of times and disappeared.

Consuming another sip of dewine, the most bitter tasting drink which tasted sweetly addictive to him since long, he said, 'so you made David's memories unreadable at instances.'

He put the glass down and walked slowly in the dark room. His black outfit swept the floor as he walked. His muddled hair further sheltered his face.

'If I say, my efforts of a little time, have not done bad in matching the magic cultivated and amended ever since.' Zolahart said to himself. 'How I believe I'm meant to be the one. The everlasting Master of the Universe.'

CHAPTER 11

✦
✦ ✦
✦

BEING AGAIN

Semester Forthe Visinus

Poemz, cruzhez, dezpairz, worriez, dreamz, adventurez; and now I bring you—bam.

Whatever I want to, I'm writing to you diary coz I am told not to tell anyone elze.

Zlout 137792 Blay (didn't have enough time to remember zen, but now I know it waz 962) Time 2.

Received a call from Zir Joz, baztard Joz, telling me zat David had been called upon, and I waz required too, "immediately" to arrive zhielded at ze Office.

I waz not even given ze time to cut off ze call, which I contemplate waz zhielded. Right from ze table I waz zeated on, I zhielded myzelf to all levelz like ordered urgently, and flew to Joz—who waz actually at "Location 2" and not in an Office.

Meeting Zolahart for ze firzt time no more appeared baffling if compared to ziz zecond encounter.

He bullied me, I don't know why ze hell iz he zo fretful about me, a young girl who hazn't yet gotten any cloze to achieving her dreamz.

Before Zolahart zhielded me in addition to my own zhield, due to which I immediately went mizzing, I obviouzly had quickly turned down one man, one woman, punched Joz and targeted on Zolahart an attack zat failed only due to him looking like ze famouz and later infamouz face zat waz on ze infoletz everyblay.

A little following time waz meant to make me realize my zituation, which when I forget every memory, I wouldn't be able to.

Zolahart, ze man ended by a zouzand oficailz, waz alive; had on purpoze went quiet to apparently have died.

Can you believe it?

Iz he going to be az powerful az Paradiz, and foolishly try to outdo him. No; I know and I hope not zo. Paradiz haz created every lone grain, and wiz one clap he can change every game.

Zolahart haz got a terrible green face; ugly hair, bad voice, and he doezn't know who I am.

It waz a fearful place however, (I, I know I'm getting getting very cluttered but I can't be clearer.) Zere were bizarre lightz, green and dirty fog, hateful foodz, n zpiritz definable by a combination of all ze above adjectivez.

Zolahart zaid to me, 'You are in ze end momentz of your merry life.'

Having me inept in hiz zhieldz, he attacked me on my head, and I fell at once. Luckily no one elze dared to try a hand on me, but unluckily Zolahart'z attackz covered up zeir void.

A couple of timez, I collected all my energy and tried to exhibit a little audacity and fake my wellbeing; I waz hit until I couldn't do so anymore.

I lozt my memoriez in momentz when I found it zo difficult to even know where I am and what iz going on, when I couldn't open my eyez and look at ze world az Zemezter, when I couldn't even apprehend anyzing, and when I could only hear Zolahart'z laugh, and later on hiz allowance many more laughz; laughz which appeared like zuch a cacophony.

Ze next moment my mental pain melted away, only ze phyzical remained, and before I could open my eyez, I waz at Moc de Lilac.

A mocian, probably a Mocian official, watched me and offered help. But let me now tell you how having no antiquity feelz like.

I didn't know how I looked like, I didn't know why I waz watching what I waz watching, I didn't know anyone elze, ya I felt I waz hurt,

I didn't know if I ought to walk or not, I could not walk in a properly balanced way, like an infant, I wanted to be taught all I didn't know, but ze Mocian bombarded at me a number of queztion and I treaded back; suddenly ze Quixie flier carried me off.

A bright light appearz at ze end of ze Quixie flight if we crozz ze atmozphere of a celeztial body except a ztar; I had itz experience for ze firzt time but it horrified me additionally.

And due to my Mocian body, I ztarted feeling choked, fell down, felt at ze verge of dying out, but my life waz barred from coming out only by ze fact zat I waz yet not fifty.

Whatever Joz told waz retorting to my queztionz but I could not feel ze pain of not having my memoriez coz I didn't know it waz meant to be painful, becauze I didn't know what memoriez were!

Yep, however, I could devote more time to comprehend when it no more choked, when I became myzelf again, and more zo when I waz put to location 3. Well I feel zo zo mortified of myzelf for having lived ze next zo many blayz unworkably like a coward and a handicapped in it.

I did not even have a band. I will never have my 11 zlout old band again; everyone holdz one'z own forever in life. (I got a new one).

I had no perception of what forfeiture I waz in, but my mind iz of a 13 year old grown up teenager and could perceive much.

Only you can not at all find it boring to hear whatever happened for blayz in Location 3. I kept zitting, zleeping, hardly got to eat, and got to eat yukky deterring ztuff to make it hell.

I tried to attack ze guardz, to melt zem, but helping me could make zem helplezzly penalized, and anyway, zey were melt-proof.

I would run my mind to realize ze maximum, analyze ze condition, and create a happier life, a new life. I had no memoriez yet I waz Zemezter and my mind worked like it alwayz had.

Zere wazn't likelihood of doing much, but I contemplated myzelf more zan a captive. I re-experienced my indigenouz magic which I can do even while I am deprived of a band.

But before I could put zem to uze or experiment, David, my dear friend had arrived. Ze bezt zing he did, and which made me take hiz zide waz zat he gave me a pink band.

On-wearing-ze-band, I didn't know what to do. I zaid and did much, waz feeling trembled; (now my reactionz look a little funny).

Ziz ain't looking like a tiny enmity anymore.

Paradiz told David zat 'you are ze only one wiz whom I can change appearance. Wooh, I loved adventurez but not to ze extent zat my life becomez ze utmost adventure of all timez!

Anyway, it waz a terrible experience, you can't kill me before I am Zemezter Forze Visinuz 50. I am 13 and zat means I have 37 zloutz left.

I contemplate I would be much more grave and grief-ztricken had I beheld my memoriez all along. Forgetting it all made it much meeker.

CHAPTER 12

THE NEW SECRET

'Sorry,' David said. 'I'm late.'

'I thought all this would have brought a positive effect on you,' Semester replied, twittering, 'but there you are; you're late for the first time I suppose!'

'Eh . . . I don't seriously have a reply.' David said.

'I see,' Semester laughed again. 'Don't tell me Romella and Justin got the information that we are here for a walk, and that they are coming.'

'Alright,' David said, 'I won't tell you.'

'You can't mean that! I wanted to talk about something only to you.' Semester exclaimed.

'Relax,' David said, 'Romella is having her exam. She's sitting for an experator's post in Plaryzomes.'

'What!' Semester exclaimed, laughing again 'She's applying for a teaching job? In Plaryzomes? Cool. And Justin?'

'I simply told him to come later.' David answered.

'Rude! And how's your official training coming along?' Semester asked.

'Quite well,' David said, 'You know I'm the best chap in this session.'

'Of course.' Semester hummed. 'David I wanted to say I ealizat it's not . . .'

'Wait wait wait,' David said, 'We need to shield ourselves first of all.'

'Again?' We are barred from doing so.' Semester said.

'Yeah, that's why we won't do it to all the levels Sim.' David said.

'Got you.' Semester said, smiling. 'I love adventuring anyway.'

'Shield me so that no one can hear what I say, and no one can see what I do, except Semester.' David said, and disappeared.

'Okay! Shield me so that no one can hear what I say or see what I do, except David.' Semester repeated after David and saw him stand again next to her. 'So the officials are training you well,' she said.

'Yes,' David replied, 'And the last phase of my training—to tour an inhabited planet of own choice—has given me the chance to get to Moc de Lilac. Very soon, may be tomorrow.'

'For how long?'

'For one blay.' David said.

'One blay according to us?' Semester asked.

'No!' David said, 'one blay according to the respective planets. You know one blay of ours is the same as ten Mocian blays, and one slout the same as hundred slouts of their put together. You want me to come back or not!'

'Hmm. Great,' Semester said, 'It's not that bad you see. I mean, they quite resemble our features, the Mocians. At least the one I saw. Not very colourful and funny. I mean, had it been somewhere else that they would have put me after my memories would have been scrubbed off, I would have lost my mind permanently. It's possible.'

'Wasn't funny. You were saying something you ealizat.' David came to the point.

'Oh . . . ya.' Semester said, thoughtfully. 'I ealizat it's not gonna be over so easily.'

'Wasn't funny again. Have you recovered fully?' David asked.

'Neither of them were meant to be funny.' Semester said.

'You can't be serious that it needs ealization to say this,' David explained. 'It's obvious! It's not going to be easy at all. We are really, really going to have this as an essential part of our life. Because he— is eternal now. And end and eternity are-'

'-the final things.' Semester completed.

'We need to be safe, Sim, if we are to beat it.' David said, very serious now.

'Ya.' Semester nodded, many sufferings flashing back in her mind. 'Er what? Beat it?'

'Yeah.' David said.

Semester blinked a coupled of times, and said, 'You mean just the two of us?'

'Well, until we don't urgently need Sir Paradis.' David said.

'Hmm.' Semester said, fortified. 'Of course I want to be safe!'

'Yeah that's the first thing,' David said. 'The next thing is we will find out how to weaken him how to beat him.'

'What . . .' Semester mumbled, 'how unimaginable is that. Well yes that's what I wrote in my diary. That's what I want. Just actually talking about doing s feels different.'

'I know where the two prohibited books are.' David commenced.

'What?' Semester baffled, 'Good.'

'Yes.' David said.

'Yes?' Semester repeated.

'Yeah.' David said.

'No,' Semester said, 'we are not stealing them.'

'We are . . . . Yeah stealing them.' David said, attentively.

'Okay. Some other time.' Semester said.

'After I come back.' David declared.

'Where are they?' Semester asked.

'Well there's sadly no address,' David said, 'nor can you reach them by simply picking up the Quixie Flier by a "take me to the prohibited books." We'll have to literally walk more than half the way.'

'What?' Semester screeched, 'Okay, but there must be the address to the rest half of the way?'

'Yeah,' David told, 'the nearest address to one of the books is Hexas one, and to the other book is the Ester galaxy.'

'Oh my god!' Semester exclaimed, frightfully, 'Hexas one? Is it just my fear, or do I really recollect what we read about the Hexas? Is it the degree one prison or three?'

'One. The worst. Its Hexas three that is the least problematic.' David said.

'But you said it's just half way down. The destination will be well away.' Semester held.

'I also tried to read a little more about the books,' David told, 'but the reality is that not much has ever been stated about them.'

'Just that they are prohibited, contain unheard magic wiles and that Paradis wrote them before he ended? I mean before he faked that he ended.' Semester asked.

'Almost that,' David said, 'although, I came to know about a little more relavant stuff for our plan. The Prohibited books were originally a unity, it was a single book. The first Master of the Universe after Paradis, Sir Ahliz, was a great and trusted disciple of Paradis. And he didn't want the book to be misused. He cast some sort of magic on the book to make anyone who spotted it to feel strong repulsion to it. But the magic miscarried and made the books attract anyone who saw them. He kept the book with him throughout his life, safely in the Senate. But he never looked at it again as a token of regret for having tempered incorrectly with it. However, before he ended, he decided to pass it on to his own disciple and told him to dump it permanently as the book was now next to a curse. As he opened the chamber where he had kept the book, both the men's eyes fell on it, and both of them were attracted to the extent that they soon were literally fighting; and the book tore into two halves. Sir Ahliz, being the Master of the Universe and a direct disciple of Paradis, further struggled for the other half, and then dumped the two parts in separate locations, with permanent orders for prohibited reopening of their respective chambers. He ended, but the books have never been seen again.'

'You know too much,' Semester said, 'in fact you know everything about the books! Don't you? Because nothing beyond that has happened with those books afterwards.'

'Well all this information is available easily to anyone.' David said, 'what is new is that I know where the two chambers are.'

'And how do you know?' Semester whispered.

'I am a to-be official.' David answered.

Justin and Romella appeared together nearby.

'Then you're such a betraying official!' Semester said to David. 'Are you a disciple of Joz?'

'Shut up.' David said. 'So you think all this prohibited books plan is worth our time? Is it going to help us?'

'I really think so.' Semester said.

'Unshield me then.' David said, smiling.

'Unlock me.' Semester followed.

As the pink shield visibly broke down, Justin stared at David and Semester with murderous stares, while Romella looked stunned.

'How dare you shield yourself yet again?' Justin bellowed.

'We're safe.' David said. 'And you, little scoul, did you just lose your memories?'

'Shut your mouth!' Romella squeaked, 'I still look to you like a dumb creature of the size of a handful? I am 12 now!'

'Then by now, you must have stopped feeling bad about this old name that David addresses you with, Romi.' Semester explained.

Romella stared all the three friends of hers one by one, continuing to have a assaulted look on her face, and then said, 'Let's walk.'

'Is it okay to not to tell these two anything about it?' Semester asked David.

David gave Semester a stern look.

'Which thing now?' Romella questioned.

Justin remained indifferent, which meant he was really fed up and annoyed.

'You keep things to yourself.' Romella slurred.

'Well, Sir Atz has told us to keep it confidential,' David said, realizing that it had to be stopped before the officials, who would definitely be keeping an eye on them constantly, start interrogatin them about the secret, 'it's about who had abducted Semester.'

'Can we go for some food instead?' Semester proposed.

'Yeah, that's better.' David confirmed.

'I'm not coming.' Justin said, preparing to leave.

'What? Justin, what happened?' Semester said, while Romella and David simply looked on.

'Back to home.' Justin said, and disappeared.

CHAPTER 13

CLUELESS EXCURSION

Rodge had been taken home after being granted a short leave from the Plaryzomes boarding-house to be at home with his reconciled family. He had not got enough time to talk to his sister since she had come back.

Rodge 6 was then around half the age of Semester, but seemingly had double her sensibility, according to conventional perceptions about sensibility and was severely annoyed with her. He had more control over the family's security and outside issues than Semester. He was also clearly outstanding in households and foods while Semester had always remained a stranger to these.

However, Semester was the cute charmer and was more sought and cared after. So, in case Rodge had to stay for some more time outside of Plaryzomes, he needed her help.

'Rodge says he would like to stay here toblay,' Semester said to her mother.

'No.' Rose decided fast, and as usual.

'Mummy please!' Rodge bawled, ready to lie down and roll.

'It's just a matter of one blay!' Semester spoke for Rodge again.

'What happened?' Peter said, in a normal way, as noise and wildness was a part of this house.

'I don't know anything,' Rodger shouted, 'I just won't go back toblay.'

Staying at Plaryzomes was a part of the discipline of Plaryzomes. It was believed that although spirits were the most distinguished and supreme living beings, becoming an efficient one was a skill and needed to be taken seriously.

The situation was that Peter was not in the mood to impress Rose by taking her side, and Rose was left alone in her opinion.

So, Rodge stayed at home.

'Came back alive?' Roger said by pushing her aside on her own bed, signalling that he would sleep there, 'and with memories too!'

'I didn't have my memories when I arrived.' Semester mumbled, making cute sound to divert Rodger's mind to her hair. Rodge had an inborn trait of being over obsessed by hair, as if they were his prohibited books.

'This is not a joke okay Semester,' Rodge said, confirming how serious he was.

'Umm . . .' Semester slurred.

Semester began explaining to Rodge what had happened, and that she possibly had no control over it. Rodge commanded her to be careful thereafter, to which Semester smiled. To Rodge this smile meant that she was going to be careful, but to Semester, it was reminiscent of the next plan. she had formulated with David a little time back. She told Rodge that David was going to Moc de Lilac as the last phase of his training for becoming an official.

At the end, Rodge fell asleep, his hands draped in Semester's hair.

Early next blay, Rodge was ready to get back to Plaryzomes. 'Semester!' Rose called loudly from the other room early blay.

'Yes!' Semester replied, beginning to move there.

'Yes, let me tell her,' Peter was saying to Rose.

'What?' Semester asked.

'Received a call from the Head Office.' Rose angrily said.

'What for?' Semester said.

'You again shielded yourself with David, you want to be safe or not?' Rose thundered.

'We didn't shield ourselves,' Semester said. 'We just, wanted to talk about something.'

'Why?' Rose said. 'What was it that no one should listen to you? What was it?'

'Sir Atz himself has told David and me to keep a secret about something.' Semester said.

'Really?' Rose said.

'Yes. You can ask him.' Semester said.

'Okay then,' Peter said, 'there is an on-going discussion on whether you two should be allowed to shield yourself or should be made temporarily incapable of doing so.'

Semester didn't say anything. She tried not to look alarmed.

'Of course they want to divest you from doing so because it still seems that you are unaffected by the recent disasters,' Peter further went on, 'and they are also considering not to take any such action because at times you might require to shield yourself in defence.'

'Why don't you simply understand you are wandering with your life spinning on your palm!' Rose shouted. 'You will not go with David now.'

'What does it mean!' Semester argued. 'Don't be over confident, okay! And by the way, David is going for the last part of his training, most probably toblay. And he is going to Moc de Lilac, do you know that? DON'T GO WITH DAVID! Do you know who brought me back? How can people be so sick!'

'Okay, we know.' Peter said, turning to Rose, he continued, 'What can we do now; destiny is also something. Bravery has its own consequences.'

Rodge had also entered the room now. 'What happened?' he whispered to Semester, to which she just nodded to her, telling him to be silent.

'But it looks like there is no effect on her!' Rose said, 'I can't understand all . . .'

'It's okay,' Peter said, 'these children must have definitely become more sensible. There is something that the Head of the galaxy has told them to keep something as a secret, may be it's related to their safety. They might just be following that.'

'What happened?' Rodge asked, louder this time.

'You are not required to have that explained to you right now.' Peter said, as usual transferring his anger on Rodge, who just generally happened to interject at the wrong time.

'Are you ready?' Rose asked Rodge.

'Ya.' Rodge dully answered.

Just then Semester received a call from David, 'David's calling me,' she said and came back to her room.

'Yes David.' She said.

'I have to move before time two; can you see me before I go?' David asked her.

'You're going now?' Semester asked.

'Yeah, can't you see I'm ready?' David said.

'Yes I can . . . I got to tell you something,' Semester said.

'What is it?' David asked.

'Nothing great,' Semester answered, keeping in mind the officials who might check the conversation, and thus acting to be perfectly okay with the new issue that had cropped up.

A few hundreds of trainees had amassed near the Head Office of the Atz galaxy, waiting to execute the last task before they became the new batch of officials under the Head of their galaxy. A lot of security measures had been taken and no one other than one family member per trainee was endorsed.

David flied back to Semester shortly before the addressing by the Head, Sir Atz.

Semester had been waiting in Romella's house.

'They'll be furious if they find you are tempering with the discipline to the very last moment possible,' Semester said in hushed tones to David.

'May be, but this is important too.' David said.

'My mum received call from the Head Office. They're discussing about whether to make us unable to shield ourselves at all.' Semester informed.

'And you didn't guess they would have called my home too?' David asked.

'They did?' Semester muffled.

'Yeah,' David said, 'now listen. It's completely okay. Just be ready.'

'Oh . . . kay.' Semester said.

'Just be ready,' David repeated, 'And don't invite any trouble while doing so.'

'Eh . . . hmm,' Semester said, 'I got you.'

'See you then,' David said, hugging her.

'Justin didn't come,' Romella mused, feeling desolated.

David posed a little uncomfortable smile and said, 'It's okay. My pet scoul is here.'

Romella knocked David on that and stepped back when he came forward to hug her.

'See you.' Semester said.

'Take me back to the Head Office,' David said. The Quixie flier immediately in took him and ran fast towards its destination; its blue colour changing to pink towards the end of the journey, which meant David was being verified on whether he could enter the shielded place he was going to.

'Where were you supposedly!' Jonas said, looking in an impasse between fulfilling the formalities for David's tour and taking care of his whereabouts.

'To Semester. Dad,' David replied, 'you could have seen, we hadn't shielded ourselves.'

Jonas stared at David as there was not much time left for an argument. Then feeling provoked, he displayed the form to David.

'You see what is written here. There are five such sets of brochures.' Jonas said, reading out one of them, 'The trainee will be withdrawn and if required, suitably punished if involved in any undesirable activity, if found being undisciplined, if found unfocussed from the training motive, if found uncreative in the tour, if found violating any regular spiritual rules.'

'Yeah,' David said, looking everywhere except at Jonas.

Jonas rolled the frames and sighed. 'All the best.'

'Thanks.' David said, smiling.

Everyone assembled systematically on the field to listen to Sir Atz's final speech.

Amidst lowering of noise and movements, Sir Atz appeared floating above everyone else in the arena.

'Good time,' he wished everyone.

'Good time,' roughly half the crowd replied.

Atz smiled and continued, 'I would try not to take much time. It is a pleasure to meet my young likely employees. It's been a long time that I myself made such a trip as a trainee. We all go to bizarre places where we usually find ourselves very uncomfortable. We also carry the fear of running into troubles of the likes stated in the brochures. But most of us come up with learning very much about governance . . .'

'Why the hell did he tell us not to mention Zolahart to anyone . . .' David muttered.

Sir Atz continued his speech, with the Chief Experator of Paryzomes, Sir Laurins standing closes to him and winking.

'What is the Head of Plaryzomes doing here!' David said, baffled.

Sir Laurins was occasionally interrupted by possible local official or attendants, who showed him certain frames. Laurins appeared to be resolving their queries which meant he was participating in the Outer Senate's issues.

'Dad!' David couldn't stop himself from asking, 'what could Sir Laurins be doing here?'

'Sir Laurins?' Jonas rose up a little to find where Laurins stood. 'I can't guess. He could have some link to a part of the training procedure.'

'. . . you don't have to worry about.' Sir Atz was smiling while delivering the speech. 'As and when you reach your respective planets, you will automatically transform into just one of the substrates. Your body will start functioning like you were an inhabitant. But it does not have an impact on your age, you will still live for exact fifty slouts.'

'Look at his body language,' David continued, 'and look where he is standing, as if he is the personal secretary of Sir Atz.'

Everyone clapped and the activities augmented again. Sir Atz could be seen receiving the biddings of the crowd and proceeding towards the Outer Senate.

David tried to find out where Sir Laurins would go now but the crowd and activities barred the view.

'See you, soon.' David said.

'See you son.' Jonas replied, hugging David.

'Not here!' David said, 'Er, well, okay! Okay! Bye.'

'Bye.'

Trainees started departing into their Quixie Fliers. The crowd began to diminish as boys and girls disappeared to reach their chosen planets.

'Take me to Moc de Lilac.' David said. He disappeared as the Quixie Flier engulfed him. He was anxious about what would be the first sight he would see, about what Semester had experienced. Before he could imagine anymore, an extremely bright light excelled and flooded the whole of the Quixie Flier. Its blaze hurt David's eyes before it had reached its peak luminescence and he tightly shut his eyes, his hands covering them for further defence in a reflex.

When he felt okay to do so, he removed his hands and slowly opened his eyes. It took some time for the vision to get clear, to get rid of the sheen of the Quixie, and he stood where he was trying to open his eyes; looking like he was trying to tear them apart.

It slowly cleared and David found himself standing in front of a blue sea of clear water on the front; noises unheard before and creatures unseen before at the back. Then he looked at his own reflection on a nearby trolley, and was taken aback.

'I don't look better,' he muttered, 'but Sim was right, it's pretty much the same features.'

He felt he now needed to breathe unavoidably and that he felt a weird hunger in his stomach. He checked if his band was still intact, and it was.

Trying to cross the roads, he nearly bumped onto a car.

'Is the whole planet a playground!' He cursed the vehicle, 'Why would all of them ride small boxes'

He landed in front of a restaurant. But merely strained his eyes on the name board.

'Charlie' ... Re ... taurant?' He surprisingly said to himself. 'What could that symbol mean!'

After deciding not to ask anyone about it, he entered.

He noticed he was supposed to sit at one of the tables. He took to a corner seat and a man in white uniform handed him over a leaflet, said 'Sir' and went.

David picked up the leaflet and opened it.

'Breakfa...t' David said, looking perplexed again, 'What is this symbol? Lunch, ...nack, dinner, drink... Oh, I get it, they use it in place of a z.'

Another waiter came back, 'What would you like to have, sir?'

'Er, what's the best out here?' David asked.

'We make the city's best Chicken Nuggets and Fries in town sir,' the waiter blabbered as if he had crammed it up.

'Eh, well, I would like to have both of them, then,' David said, 'but what do you use, you know, to make them?'

'I'm sorry sir, we're not allowed to let out the recipe.' The attendant said.

'No, I mean, what's the major ingredient?' David asked.

'Chicken and potato, respectively, sir,' the waiter said.

'Ohhhh! I see I see. Thanks a lot. Bring it.' David said, faking a smile.

The waiter too faked a smile and said, 'Your welcome, sir. I just felt you needed a little help, but we have self service here.'

'Okay,' David said, 'What is it?'

'Sir, you will have to come up to the counter and order your choice.'

'Oh, alright.' David said, getting up and following the waiter to make sure he went to the counter, but thankfully did not move on towards the kitchen.

'Er... can I ... could you please call the man who just mentioned to me two things you offer over here?' David asked at the counter.

The lady at the counter looked at David and called David the waiter.

'Is your name David?' David asked the waiter.

'Yes, sir,' the waiter replied, wondering if that was what he had been called for.

'Oh my god! Me too!' David exclaimed, 'I'm David!'

'Uh... that's great sir,' the waiter replied, looking fearful.

'Er, what had I just ordered?' David whispered to him.

'Chicken nuggets and fries, sir,' the waiter said, looking angry now.

'You see?' David turned to the lady at the counter, 'it's chicken nuggets and fries.'

'Nine point eight one,' the lady said.

'Er, what?' David said.

'Nine point eight one pounds,' the lady repeated.

'What's that?' David asked.

'Do you want *chicken nuggets* and *fries* sir?' the lady said, looking redder, 'if yes, you have to pay nine point eight one pounds right now.'

'I'll catch you later,' David said, turning towards the door and then walking out of it.

'Damn!' David stubbed his foot on the road, 'I'm hungry!'

'Eleven pounds?' David heard a man say, handling over the paper sheets to another man, 'here you are, thanks.'

David walked up to the man, who looked very busy, 'Excuse me, did he just hand you over some pounds?'

'Er...yes,' the man said, looking suspiciously at David, 'why?'

'Well, can I join in your task I really need some pounds,' David said.

'Do I look like the owner of this pump to you?' the man said, continuing his work side by side, 'fifteen pounds, madam.'

'You earn a thousand dollar by a day, am I right?' David questioned.

'Only hundred per month... you know the taxation and the salary,' the man answered 'now I would like you to leave me alone.'

'Alright, it's getting dark although here,' David said, 'how much more darker will it get?'

The man jammed and stared dangerously at David.

'Got you,' David said, pacing away.

Though feeling very hungry, David couldn't arrange for himself anything to eat, and soon, he started feeling sleepy too.

'What's going on, man!' He said, sitting down on a park bench, 'Life is so difficult here.'

He looked at a distant road, and the numerous tall lightened buildings across it, and thought to himself, 'It's quite different from what I have seen till now, but, not anywhere near our buildings.'

Slowly, he lay down on the bench, being vigilant in case someone came to tell him sleeping there wasn't allowed; and soon he fell asleep.

CHAPTER 14

EDUCATIONAL COFFEE DATE

Even though the biggest link Hexas had to the strategy was that one of its three fragments lied on the way to the destination, Semester had started reading about Hexas before she started concentrating on anything else. She had to think afresh, for she had no idea of how David had planned to execute things, or whether he had planned anything at all.

She had decided to go for further experation at Plaryzomes, instead of getting a job. Unlike David, who had to rush from one task to another, she had ample of time as the higher courses had not yet started. However, a major problem was that Plaryzomes had entered the patriotic club by emphasising on the rule that only natives of its galaxy can be experated there over. Semester was the only one in her group who belonged to the Lilac, and not the Atz. The institute of her own Lilac galaxy, Iliaegazomes, where her mother was an experator, was as not well renowned as Plaryzomes. Although it was experating almost all the natives of the Lilac, but until very recently Plaryzomes had been easy on experating outsiders; so quite many opted for it over their own institute.

Through whatever was available about Hexas which unfortunately was scarce, all she could know were terrifying facts like the size and monstrosity of Bacons, the hungry gigantic animals that were left astray in all the three degrees of Hexas. There was only one rule in the Hexas, that there was no rule applicable. Anyone could do anything they liked, which only meant that the Bacons could do anything they liked. If the miseries and unseen assaults of the Hexas were avoided for a moment, the other name of Hexas could be a mental asylum.

Anyhow, Semester realised (because she wanted to realise this) that Hexas one would not be quite a problem as they *simply* had to walk past it.

Next, it seemed to her that stealing the Prohibited books was difficult as hell, and that David and she might finally land up as criminals in one of the Hexas, preferably the one they had crossed while on their way.

It would have been much better if she could contact David, because she could see more chances of landing into troubles, than getting the Prohibited books. She was doubtful about morality here, that is, she didn't know whether to continue living a life which would, sooner or later, be in danger or to push herself into danger deliberately in order to stop having to be vigilant and petrified all the time.

The deeper she thought, the scarcer the chances of triumph seemed. The prohibited books had been safe since the beginning of the ages. They were preserved by the first Master of the Universe, Sir Ahliz, a direct disciple of the God. Facts devastated her confidence like a Bacon could perish a scoul; and ultimately every thought of hers terminated visualising herself with David in Hexas one.

Now she wished she had thought much more before agreeing to the suicidal plan. She had around thirty seven slouts of her age remaining, and in case she was assigned a Hexas, she would have herself soccered and crushed for a long lifetime because even in Hexas, no one died before fifty slouts. The Location Three seemed an easy option momentarily.

Semester was gifted with indigenous skills, which on an average two in a thousand spirits possess. Such skills didn't ever require a band, enabling her to somewhat rediscover them while she was in Location three. She could instantly hallucinate or hypnotise two spirits at the same time, reaching up to three people when more accurate and in practice. Although this hypnotism had no permanent effects, which was an obvious and necessary fact. She could throw immense light as well, in whichever pattern or intensity she wanted, the maximum intensity being that of a mimic of her birth star, of which she was a spirit.

'Where are you going?' Rose asked, watching Semester going out while she came back from Iliaegazomes.

'To the library,' Semester said.

'Whaa . . .' Rose said, looking shocked as if Semester had pledged not to shield herself ever again.

David had, coincidentally, too, ended up at a library in what he now knew was Scotland. He was still hungry, had been living on water and had no means to buy anything for food; he chose to stay hungry for he knew that a Mocian blay was really far too short. When he had decided to travel and explore on what had seemed like a small planet up till now, terms like pounds, passport, visa, aeroplanes and metro were swirling his mind. So, on his part, it was the best to go for a library, which was a familiar term, to virtually travel into different places and time.

The pages looked extremely dull to David as he was accustomed to silver frames. He could not fully concentrate as he was starving.

The first topic he picked up was politics, the other name of governance on earth, and flipped from Scotland to all across the world. First of all, he came across the international map identical to how Moc de Lilac looked from outside its atmosphere. Though it was much later that he realised it was called the 'Earth'.

He felt overburdened when he realised it was quite difficult to grasp considerable information as there were an endless list of things like the nations, the political parties, the elections, the diplomacy and the corruption that glided over his mind. The international relations, currencies, trade, deals, the history of enemies and allies, and Gandhi and Mandela . . . he felt he had had enough of the topic.

'Would you like to drink some coffee, sir?' said a man with grey hair, and with heavy spectacles that appeared to David like it was the spectacles that had worn the man's face instead.

'Er, I don't have pounds,' David dully replied.

'Well, sir, I am not asking for any,' the old man smiled, and David imagined light all around his small old face, making him look like an angel. 'It's just a friendly proposal. You look tired and perplexed sir, and desperately in need of some information. I hardly find people approach the libraries these days. You see, the internet era.'

Hearing another set of unknown words, 'Cawfee please,' David simply said.

The old man gestured a smile and went off to bring the coffee.

Try how hard he may, David couldn't read a word before the old man appeared again. His hopeful eyes stared at the door. The old man's shadow appeared near the door in a couple of minutes, and moments later, he entered, but empty handed.

David looked deceived.

'The maid is just bringing it,' the old man said, reading the why-you-doing-this-to-me look on David's face. 'Gandhi . . .' The old man said after straining on one of the books so hard as if trying to spot an atom or two on its cover page.

'Ye . . . yeah,' David stammered, imagining how exactly a coffee could be.

'Great man. I have read half of the books here,' the old man said, doing something which David ultimately realised was laughing.

'Half the books! Er, in case you remember what you have read, and I, I'm sure you have experience also, cause you live here, it'll be better to ask you instead of reading the books.'

'Sure, why not.' The old man said, 'After all, I hardly get to talk to someone.'

'Well, I need to know about . . . the buildings now,' David said.

'The buildings?' the old man said, 'you are already in one. Any specifically?'

'Er, the best, you see,' David said, looking narrowly at the old man.

'You . . . you go for the seven wonders then,' the old man said, 'get up, get up to the third rack over there, there is a good book about the wonders.'

David got up, realising that the old gentleman was actually helpful. Just then, a girl entered, with coffee in a tray. She placed it on the table and David accidently picked any book from the rack and headed back. The old man, surprisingly sharp enough to observe, immediately said, 'Not that one, I think it's about the prettiest girls.'

David looked at the book he was holding, the old man was surprisingly correct, but the girls on the cover page didn't appeal to him, 'Prettiest?' he muttered to himself, 'even Romella is better.'

'I have been putting the books in the correct order since years,' the old man said, picking up the coffee mug, 'read properly and get the correct book from the correct stack.'

David hurriedly placed the pretty girls' book back on the rack, and searched for the correct book on the adjacent rack.

'The modern wonders?' David asked.

'Er, yes, yes.' The old man nodded.

David ran towards the table and extended his hand towards the mug before he was seated. But just before he could sip it, he felt it was hot, so he smile and put it back.

The old man, meanwhile showed to him a picture of the first wonder, The Great Pyramid of Giza.

'You know how distinguished it is?' The old man said, his questioning tone sounding like a whistle towards the end. 'It is the only living wonder, which was also the . . . ahem . . . ahem ahem' the old man coughed, 'the wonder of ancient times. It is four thousand years old!'

'Four thousand . . .' David muttered, calculating . . . 'just around four hundred slouts that is . . . I can't wonder . . .'

'What?' the old man looked at David from above his spectacles. 'The Taj Mahal. A perfect example of symmetrical architecture without the use of cement!'

'Well . . .' David said, sipping coffee finally, and making a weird face at its taste, wondering if the old man had tried to poison him, "anyway I can't die, and it seems to suppress my hunger somewhat", he thought. He kept drinking and the old man spoke to his content.

'I'm done with the government, the wonders, and . . . the coffee . . .' David said, 'is there an inescapable thing one should know?'

'. . . environment? Poverty? Eh . . . what kind of a question is that . . .' the old man asked. 'there are more than eight hundred living languages in a small country like Papua New Guinea, one thousand six hundred recognised ones and four hundred fifty listed ones in India, robots in Japan . . . Julius Caesar . . . literature . . . religions, gods . . . what do you want?'

David's eyes then fell on a newspaper kept on the table, 'Infolet?' he asked.

'Eh? Yeah you can call it that. Information outlet,' the old man grumbled.

Picking the infolet up, David's eyes fell on a headline:

Now officially credited as Mrs. Wright

'What does that mean?' David asked.

The old man made a suspicious 'is it already not clear' expression and then said, 'This popular actress, recently married to Wright, and now is being credited in her movies by the surname Wright, not her maiden name Jones.'

'Why?' David asked.

The old man looked at David so gravely that David wondered whether he was still looking perfectly Earthian or was beginning to look alien.

'What are you asking? more than half the women do that. This is the West though; certain eastern nations have real sexism. This is perfectly fine, perfectly acceptable and right. She might be an actress but is a wife first.'

'(They even have a term for it, sexism!!)How ridiculous and abhorrent . . . yuk!' David said, his mouth fallen open.

The old man, taken aback, blinked around six times.

'Er . . . I mean I have seen this, but don't you think the women here do not even fall in the category of the race of . . . humans. The supreme creatures on Earth are not humans, they are men. These women have no self respect. This is pathetic.'

'What's so pathetic!' The old man exclaimed, 'you talk like you are the Buddha, all of a sudden exposed to the worldly ways.'

'Ways?' David queried, 'This is total nonsense. She might be a popular whatever . . . actress, she has no self respect, and if you call this West modern and advanced, I say, try to see more clearly sir, because I think such women either have no self respect or lack affinity to open up their minds,'

'Hang on young angry boy,' the old man said, looking completely startled, 'What does a woman generally say at the wedding, that she will love and obey.'

'W-H-A-T?' David said, getting up, 'Are they pets? Do they grant their brains to museums and become useless bodies?'

'Women do have rights, there have been debates. Women may choose to not to change their surnames or to *obey*. Some are not even using their husband's name for their kids.'

'They used to? Oh man, are they machines giving birth to babies for someone else . . . ? I . . . . Oh . . . And rights . . . you sounded like they are lucky to have those rights. Debates about women's rights are just show-offs then. Rights not only mean to go out, to study, to laugh, to wear what you want or to do the job of your choice, I think it should be *being able to do right things, being able to be modern if you call yourself modern.* You are nowhere having an equal share in humanity or rights if you are more of a household than your man is, if you bloody change your . . . your surname . . . unbelievable . . . if you give birth to someone who is more somebody else's than yours; stupid ones may argue "come on, it's just by name!" Holy shit I think any such woman doesn't even deserve respect 'cause she doesn't need any. I'm feeling creepy here, thank god it's time to go,' David said, looking out of the window at the dusky skyline, thinking "*How would Semester or Romella or my mum or any other woman react if I felt like vomiting at this stuff.*"

'I think what you are talking seems secondary in these times when violence, assaults, rapes etcetera against women are still existing.

'(V-I-O-L-E-N-C-E!!!!) . . . Er, I think it originated due to the difference in physical power if Earthians ever since Earthians are existing.'

The old man, looking as if he himself got something new to think that day, said, 'Are you going now, or you need some more to read?'

'Er, nothing . . . it's enough for toblay,' David said.

'Where are you from?' The old man asked.

'What?' David said.

'Is toblay a Russian word?' the old man asked.

'Er . . . perhaps,' David said, 'thanks a lot sir. You are incredible.'

'You're a nice boy, but I suppose you developed the instinct for learning quite late, ahem ahem ahem . . . . ahem . . . . well, nothing is too late for a good quest. Have a great day.'

'Thank you sir, same to you. Takecare.' David said. It was time to finally get back after rearranging the books.

As he stepped out of the library, he took a last glance at the river, the bridge, the small buildings, the ground, the Mocians, the other Mocian creatures, the vehicles, the sky, all the strange things.

'I thought it was a small planet. It's a universe in its own self.' David thought to himself, 'Gods? Thousands of languages! And races . . . ? And sexism! I thought there was just one race over here—Mocians.'

CHAPTER 15

THE STEALTH

On his arrival back, David was supposed to submit a report on his excursion. The report was to decide the respective seniority of the new appointments.

A number of candidates had intentionally or unintentionally violated one or more rules stated in the rule lists, and had been immediately withdrawn and sent for further actions. Some had succeeded in not breaking any rules but unfortunately succeeded in nothing beyond that. Some had got useless information and all in all, whatever David had done, combined with his earlier tasks, could easily make him a senior official of a rather high rank.

All the prohibited books idea, though, was almost going to steal all the chances away. He felt that things could be easier for him if he waited to be nominated first, and if as an official he committed any misconduct, he would be in a better situation. So he decided to wait, and hoped that in the meanwhile, he would find an even better way to escape any penalty.

On the other hand, Justin continued to behave abnormally and rudely. David and Semester seemed to put in no efforts to give any explanation, and Romella, who had had no role in the secrets of the two, was alone trying to talk to him.

Romella had started taking classes as an experator in Plaryzomes. Being an ex-student of the same, she was familiar with almost all the experators, including the Chief Experator Laurins, and some students who earlier had been her juniors.

After Plaryzomes, the four were exposed again to things other than to one another. David and Semester got more time to spend with their respective families, who thought that David and Semester were now perfectly normal.

The normalcies came to an end a little before David and Semester expected them to.

David was appointed as the junior-most senior official, and that was better than most of the appointments but not at all on a par with his performance. His family and friends also did not know how to react as he had imparted a much better image to them.

Shortly, David was enraged.

Among the merry new officials in front of the iridescent golden Senate, David said angrily to his father, 'I'm not joining the office.'

'What!' Jonas said, 'You might have lacked in some aspect. As you continue your work you will find out exactly how things work out! And, there are promotions, you know that.'

Without saying anything, David went inside the Head office, the Senate, where he had to place his hands on the Fireball of Power and take his oath.

When Semester came to know about David's underachievement according to his expectations, she sensed it might affect their mission. She felt it was not the right time to congratulate him. She sat down and started reading her self-written poetry from her personal diary. It was time to make another entry in it as she was not sure if she would get the chance do it again after she tried to steal the Prohibited books.

The moment her mind wandered again to the Prohibited books, David called her.

'Hi David . . . em . . . that's great you are a senior official now,' Semester falteringly said.

'Are you ready? Looks like you have got surplus time to prepare.' David said.

'What?' Semester said, putting down her diary.

'Come here!' David loudly said, looking tensed.

'Like, you mean I should . . . get ready?' Semester asked.

'If you're talking about putting on make-up, then certainly not,' David replied roughly again.

'Okay . . .' Semester said, not forgetting to keep her diary safely back. Her father, Peter had twice read it and left remarks duly undersigned.

Thinking about not meeting any family member before leaving, she erratically flipped through the last page of the diary, where she had kept the old withered golden frame written by Paradis.

'What the hell . . .' she said, hurriedly searching her wardrobe and the shelves. 'Oh my God! Take me to David.'

"I didn't even notice it when I wrote the diary entry after I came back," she thought while travelling.

David was waiting for her just outside his house, not conventionally an ideal place for disappearing into the next adventure.

'The . . . The frame is not there . . .' Semester stammered to David.

'Which one?' David asked.

'Em . . . nothing . . . will tell you when . . . nothing . . .' Semester said, not wanting to give the officials another thing to note.

'Semester, shield yourself, if I shield you, you will be quoted as "missing" which will be a bigger problem. Shield me to all levels,' David said.

'Shield me to all levels,' Semester said as soon as they got shielded, 'The frame written by Paradis, it's missing!'

'I'm so sorry I forgot to tell you, it's with the officials, they had searched your house while you were missing,' David said, 'Take us near Moc de Lilac.'

'How can you forget telling me about it!' Semester said, 'So, we're okay with it? And did they come to know about anything? And why are we going near Moc de Lilac!'

'They reached the place after unravelling what was written on the paper, but did nothing beyond that,' David said. 'And I just wanted to go away from my house. Earth . . . er Moc just came to my mind. Now listen to me, we're not stealing the books.'

'What!' Semester shrieked, 'what have you called me here for, and why did you shield then!'

'Okay give me a plan then to get away with the books without getting into trouble. Even if we steal them, the suspicion would be largely on us because we have shielded ourselves.'

'But the books are so well protected, and also unseen that no one will even notice if they have been taken away.'

'Right now, you take this frame and this ink,' David said, handing her over one of the two silver pages he had brought and an inked lead, 'If it is quite safe and worriless to get the book, which it definitely won't be, then bring it. But remember, there may be a truth test later also. So just write down whatever you can. You go to the prohibited book on the way to Hexas, there is a rough map on the backside. I will go to the other one. We can't go together for the same book as we will both be attracted to it, and start fighting.'

'Copy down the book! What if it's a huge book!' Semester exclaimed, 'you must be kidding me, you can't make such a ridiculous plan!'

'Of course you have a better one, don't ya?' David mocked, 'The way I am suggesting, the book will remain at its place and we won't run into many troubles, we won't be accused of committing crimes at least.'

'Very well, then we don't know how many have read the book till now, because they would have just shielded themselves, read the book, and went off, no?'

'Well then I rather say, the prohibited books have been secure since ancient ancient anciennnnt times and so who are we to reach them? We can't.' David said.

'Doing simply anything will mean putting the whole life at stake,' Semester explained, 'even if we never unshield ourselves again, the officials will end us prematurely. Man! I can't believe it we are already shielded and still thinking of a plan! They had already warned us not to shield ourselves again.'

'Now . . . better do as I say.' David said.

'No.' Semester said, 'I talked to someone in the Office while you were in the Moc de Lilac. I asked them that they were seemingly not doing anything in my kidnap case, nor was there any scope of doing anything, so what are they hiding Zolahart's reality for? They said the government works in such and such a way behind the scenes and not everything is to be let out. Right now, we just need to blackmail the Head or, if not getting that high, someone in his office, that I not them, we have full right of trying any crook way for our safety if it does not harm anyone.'

David clapped, 'Blackmailing the Head? Have you lost your mind? And what do you think? We will unshield ourselves and go to the Head office and blackmail them, and they will circle around us and applaud while we disappear again?'

'We will drop a letter at the Office,' Semester said.

'Miss Semester Forthe Visinus,' David said, 'the prohibited books are a universal heritage which are lawfully prohibited, stealing them with the excuse of your security serves no purpose. You have no proof of it having any or only relation with your safety. Thank you.'

'Okay Mister Officer,' Semester said. She sat down on the invisible floor and started thinking. David started wandering nearby, running his mind.

Suddenly, they saw something coming towards them at a good speed. It was not shiny and had a strange figure.

'What is it?' Semester asked David.

'No idea.' David said.

The object got closer at a fast rate and looked bigger and bigger.

'It's a spaceship! Careful . . . Take us where we should be!' David yelled and just as the spaceship was about to thrash them, they vanished.

'Can you hear me?' the pilot cosmonaut signalled back to earth, 'We just saw something. Angels strikingly of the same appearance as reported in 1884 by the Soviet just vanished in front of our eyes. It could have been a collision.'

Before David, and more so Semester, could recover, they found themselves in "the place they should" have been at. They found themselves next to a crowd of a number of men, women, children, youth, and old spirits, near a local office.

'Now what's this?' Semester said, angrily scouring her muddled hair.

'No idea.' David said.

'I will go and check,' Semester said, getting up.

'Don't,' David said, 'you might keep your shield hit a dozen times before the officials break it.'

'Then?' Semester said.

'Float just above them,' David winked.

'You go then, I'm much more worried about other things,' Semester said.

'Alright,' David said, floating towards the crowd, higher and higher.

'There is no good in putting everything at stake,' Semester muttered, watching David floating above the crowd, his ears carefully overhearing what was going on. 'Everything will be lost, whatever we have till now . . . even the future. I'm simply going back.'

David ran back towards Semester at triple the speed he had went.

'Sim!' he called on much before he reached near her.

'What!' Semester screamed, irritably.

David stopped in front of her, and said, 'One of the Prohibited books is already stolen. It's not there.'

CHAPTER 16

ROMELLA'S TWO FOES

'**K**eep your hands off me,' David said, authoritatively to an attendant.

'He'sanofficer,' a fellow attendant hurriedly muttered to the attendant.

'Sorry sir,' the attendant said, pacing backwards.

Semester stood silently next to David. They had reached David's immediate senior official and unshielded themselves.

'I am an official and that gives me an advantage of having an immediate truth test. We're not lying and we have nothing to do with the lost prohibited book.'

Actually having an advantage, David and Semester followed the officer and a few others to a separate room.

'Miss Semester is not an official and she can not overlook the truth test of Sir David,' the attendant said. 'Please wait outside, miss.'

'Hmm,' Semester said, not reciprocating a very pleasant look.

The others entered the room and shut the door behind them. Semester stood next to the shut door.

Thereafter a man came running towards the room and knocked twice.

Semester wondered if an attendant could commit a disruption like that.

The attendant opened the door and the man went inside.

Semester couldn't hear the conversations inside the room. Someone with his face covered stood next to her, and as the attendant opened the door, he hurried away, pushing Semester slightly on his way.

'Hey!' she said, not currently in the mood to follow and argue with the unknown person. 'Why does he wear so much on his face that makes him blind . . . ', she muttered.

In a short while, everyone started coming out of the room one by one.

David came out too, shaking hands with his senior.

'Sorry for the inconvenience, miss,' the officer said to Semester.

'Em, it's okay Sir,' Semester said.

'Also, sir,' David said to his senior, 'every spirit has the right to talk in private, you know what I mean. Semester and me are not involved in any wrongdoings and the previous issues with us are well over. So, like any other we would like to have the right of shielding our conversations whenever we like. I would like it to be as quick as possible.'

'Oh David don't you know you definitely have the right now,' the Officer said. 'You're right. The issues are well over and you are just to receive the written notice.

'Thanks, sir,' David said, looking proud that his decision to become an Officer was his ticket to authorised mischief.

'What happened?' Semester asked David as soon as the Officer turned.

'The issue of the stolen book has critically aired. The enquiry revealed that the prohibited book has been missing for around a slout, so that proves we didn't steal it a little while ago.' David said.

'What? A slout?' Semester said. 'David . . . was it Zolahart?'

'. . . really guess so, now shut up! However,' David said, lowering his voice, 'What is astonishing is that a heritage of the like of the Prohibited book, was missing from its "secure" place since a slout, and no one knew!'

'But, what about us?' Semester said. 'We were talking about our safety. Does our discussion go to waste? Are we now doing nothing?'

'Leave your higher studies idea, Sim,' David said. 'Join instead the Interviewing Bureau of the Infolet Department. You will probably also enjoy the benefit of staying in the same office as Justin; because you're asking too many questions!'

'Justin. Did you talk to Justin?' Semester asked.

'Ask me, did Justin talk to me,' David replied.

'Okay, what are we doing right now?' Semester asked.

'I don't know about you, I'm going back home,' David said.

'What a pathetic blay!' Semester shrieked. 'This is awful!'

'Relax,' David said.

'Yeah, right. I'm really upset. See you then,' Semester said.

'Hey, now wait,' David said.

'See you,' Semester said. 'By the way, do let me know when we have the right to talk in private. Need to tell you something.'

'Well, the officer just told me we already can,' David said.

'So, I . . . need to talk you know, about something,' Semester said.

Semester and David shielded themselves immediately and went out of the office.

'You told me you found it weird to see Sir Laurins with Sir Atz at your ceremony. Romella told me, whenever she goes to see him, he asks a lot about you and me. She said it was okay in the beginning but now it's getting too much. She senses it rather as an enquiry.'

'I see,' David said, 'Sir Atz has found a new friend, and he's spying on us. But why? He knows everything. He scanned my whole brain in the truth test.'

'May be he found Paradis in your memories,' Semester said, 'and he wants to reach Him through us.'

'Yes,' David said, 'tell Romella not to tell Sir Laurins anything. Well, though she herself doesn't know much. Anyway, we have more important things to be discussed here than Sir Laurins.'

'But we can sense this silence . . . and its indirect relevance to us . . . something is being planned out behind the scenes, and we are stagnant. No, no one's gonna help us and if we just think about "being safe", let me tell you that's not sufficient.' Semester said. 'And anyway, it's not like everyone out here is simply living their life like they appear to. So we are no more kids now.'

'You stole my words,' David said, pointing to spirits around them, 'just in case we are able to look into the lives of that man or this woman, or that quiet looking girl over there, they all will be found to be engaged in one or the other thing they simply do not share. That's what that we were born out of stars for.'

'This is simply ridiculous that we are discussing our spiritual rights, David,' Semester said. 'The behaviour of others towards us and the recent activities that happened to us has made us to give second thoughts to our nature! Our . . . our ways!'

'You're right.' David said, 'I promise you, Sim, next time anyone tries to disrespect us or make us feel this way, we are going to lodge a complaint.'

'Yeah!' Semester mused, 'I wonder why we never thought of it before.'

'The prohibited book is not all that we can find a refuge in,' David said, 'and don't worry; I'm not saying so because I'm afraid. I really feel so.'

'There are going to be many, I'm sure, nut yet I can't think of one as of now,' Semester said.

'Yeah that's not a big deal, there are many ways,' David said.

'So we are going to fabricate new magic now?' Semester said. 'I'm afraid we can't count on this solution as it does not guarantee anything.' David said, 'but yes, we need to focus on our combat skills. I think we will have to have a face off.' 'Well, okay, but I hope neither of us gets injured, or it will bring about unfavorable change...'

'The really hostile spells and attacks shouldn't be cast fully.' David explained, 'For example if you are to break my hand don't do it, just say half the spell, it will be understood that I stood weak at that point and that i would have really lost it had it been Zolahart in your place.'

'I have an edge over you,' Semester winked, 'I have indigenous magic you know.'

Ignoring that, David said, '...and we will partially shield ourselves for protection.'

'When is it?' Semester asked.

'Tomorrow,' David replied.

Not having performed extraordinarily in the exam, Romella had got two choices for the subjects she wanted to teach. She had to take a few demo classes on both for a few blays and ultimately choose one subject with which she felt more comfortable. After taking classes in both the subjects; namely "Eons of History" and "Laws and logics of Para science", she finally chose "Eons of History" and headed for the Chief experator Laurins' room to report to him what she would be teaching and that it was now time for him to appoint someone else for the other subject she hadn't chosen.

Experator Laurins' Office was a tall tower which had three rooms at the top and was hollow down the height. A colourful cloud spiralled around it, hugging it like a creeper; its glittering reflections energising the otherwise dull look of the iron tower. She stepped on to the cloud, which did its job by carrying her upward through its spiral course. She meanwhile searched for some document in her bag, in case she might need it. The cloud stopped lifting her once she reached the door. She looked up and entered the non-glamorous cabin.

Sir Laurins was not present in the first room. She uttered in her low voice, 'Sir Experator...'

She stepped inside. The chamber was never left open until he himself was present inside, so Romella headed to the second and then walked towards the last one in a hurry. Her eyes then fell on something under a drawer which stopped her like she was jinxed. Her eyes stared at it and she turned to her left and walked faster towards it. She opened the door like she meant to break it down, and saw a book. She picked it up.

Someone tapped on her shoulders and but she didn't turn. Then she got hit severely and the book fell from her hands. She lifted her head up and ordered her hair to one side.

It was Sir Laurins, who now held the book behind him such that Romella could see it no more.

'I'm ...sorry..' Romella said, looking perplexed about her behaviour, 'Er...I...came to...I didn't mean to temper with your documents, I...was here to tell you that I would like to teach History.'

'You just made...damn!' Laurins said.

Better late than never, Romella finally realised what had just happened. 'Was that...the Prohibited book! You stole it! The officials are gonna be here now!'

'Thankfully, my whole Office takes complete care of privacy, and is not so easily available to the Officials. Romella, I don't want to be a fleeing criminal image. Trust me, and don't tell anyone what happened. Well in fact I shouldn't trust you like that. It's a time for quick decisions.'

'Stay there!' Romella shouted in what was the highest volume of her in her lifetime.

Not having another choice, Laurins prepared to leave.

'Stop!' Romella shouted again, holding her band, but someone suddenly ran towards her form the first room's door that was beside her, and pushed him. Not ready for this, she fell down and Laurins had obviously escaped without having any trouble from Romella's side.

She saw someone with covered face, the one who pushed her, with a sheet wrapped loosely around the whole body, vanishing.

She got up and ran towards the door, not even concerned about carrying her own bag along. She stepped on the cloud, sobbing and ran down on her own effort, not waiting for the cloud to drop her down.

Below, a number of students and her colleagues were waiting for her.

She stopped, not being sure about what she should do.

As the crowd was eager to have her amidst them, she said, 'Take me to David.'

CHAPTER 17

DARING SOULS

There was a very tense environment as David, Romella and Semester silently sat in David's cabin. David was not a very senior Official and he had limited authority in the investigation.

'It's a shame,' David said, 'Laurins stole it, and despite his being so close to Sir Atz. He must have taken an idea of the security and all while he wandered around the Outer Senate.'

'But who's this somebody who pushed Romella!' Semester said, 'and does Laurins know him?'

'I really don't have any clue who that was,' Romella said. 'That person had covered the face and the whole body... very well. I can't even tell if it was a boy or a girl or a man or a woman...and I...David I don't want any interrogation...I came here directly to you because of two reasons. One, I hate to be a part of any crime mystery, and secondly, because it might be related to you, because Sir Laurins often asked me about how you both were doing.'

'Wait-a-minute,' Semester said, 'I saw someone like that in the Office. David...when you were having your truth test, and that attendant came and told you that the book had been stolen a slout ago, there was someone with covered face I noticed. Someone's really spying on us, it's related to us, and I'm sure your office is shielded, David?'

'Yeah it is.' David said, 'You really saw someone? You think both of you being unable to see the face of two strangers makes them both the same stranger? You are being sure that you saw the same because you couldn't see the face?'

'It can make sense, David,' Semester said, 'how many do you find dressed that way.'

'You still want to waste your time? And Romi, just go back home, at most there will be one interrogation but I promise you not more than that. The Officials do need an enquiry and you are the only witness, so come on, okay?'

'Okay...' Romella said.

'I need to take leave from the Office,' David said, 'Go, Romi!'

'..Uhh..yes. Are you sure I won't be...' Romella said.

'Yeah yes you are safe from chaos, see you, take care,' David said, wrapping up her affair.

'Okay,' Romella said, slowly getting up, a little unwilling to miss the further discussion.

Watching her step out of the door and shut it back, David continued, 'I can't handle the office and my endangered life at the same time.'

Semester did not respond to this at all. David looked at her and then put aside a few cluttered frames on his desk.

'Where are you going now?' Semester asked.

'To get the leave!' David answered.

'Shall I go back home? And how would I manage my studies?' Semester said, 'They're starting in around ten blays.'

David paused at the door, and then pursed his lips, confusedly looking at Semester, and went out.

Semester picked up one of the hundreds of frames on David's table. 'Euthanasia appeal..', she read. It was an application about the next meeting on the appeal for mercy killing by a man who had lost his right hand and had a broken neck as a result of an attack made by yet unknown enemies. She went through a little and then muttered, 'nonsense.'

'Exactly, nonsense...what are you talking about though?' David said, entering the cabin again.

'You are back even before I could leave,' Semester said, putting down the frame. 'That man isn't getting his neck fixed and is giving up very easily.'

'Who?' David said, 'Oh I see. There are all kinds of them. Well may be he's afraid of another attack. And the reality is that he has no one to look after. But you could have instead cursed the attackers.'

'You got the leave?' Semester asked.

'No, some nonsense has cropped up,' David said, '...my boss said there is some urgent work and we all will have to do overtime. Taking leave is an absurd question right now.'

'Hmm?' Semester said, 'So you don't have the right to take leave? That's ridiculous.'

'Miss Semester Forthe Visinus,' David's boss said from the door, 'Kindly stop instigating my junior and leave this Office, there is an emergency.'

'Er, well sure Officer I will but I think you could try not to sound so rude,' Semester said.

'I seriously don't have time to think about how I sound,' the Officer continued, 'The other Prohibited book is in danger, and guess we know who is trying to steal it this time...well, I better say who *are* trying to steal it this time... I would personally consider letting go of the book to anyone from Salt to Satan, but not these thieves.'

'What...what is it?' David asked, looking alarmed. 'We will surely let you know as you immediately follow me to the Outer Senate, Mater David,' the Officer said,' and Miss Semester, I want this to remain a top secret,' turning swiftly and leaving the room.

David immediately followed his boss, not even looking at Semester before leaving.

'Sir...' David called after the boss.

'Keep walking David,' the boss said, walking at a running speed. He turned to the right and then to the left, and then to a narrow corridor that David had never seen in the Local Office where he himself worked. The corridor now looked more like a tunnel, with new tunnels making their way like branches from the left and from the right, even to the ceiling. David kept following the boss quickly. The tunnel opened up to a hall which appeared to have everyone already present inside except David and his boss.

'This isn't the outer Senate,' David said.

'Well yes,' the boss replied, getting instantly engrossed in his work.

A group of around two hundred men and women, probably official soldiers, marched at a distance and then disappeared.

'What's going on?' David asked, 'Are we having a war with another galaxy?'

The boss finally looked at David, 'No.'

'Then why did so many soldiers...'

'We need even more,' the boss said, 'More than lakh souls... bloody souls...those non magical, non spiritual beggars have devouringly attacked the Prohibited book. They are fighting hands on like fools, because they ain't got any magic. It will be a...well you know what it means. It's...well...They'll be killed I swear they'll be killed!'

David jammed where and how he was. 'That's quite a chance, well, is it?' he muttered to himself.

'Now will you stand here or get yourself to work?' his boss shouted at him from a crowded distance.

'I will...get to work,' David said, take me near Hexas one.'

The Quixie Flier obeyed David, who had only a rough remembrance of the way to the Prohibited book safe. As the blue walls of the Quixie flier began to fade, the roars of Bacons were getting audible.

'I-just-have-to-pass-by,' David consoled himself.

As he landed near Hexas one, he saw for the first time the first degree Hexas, the sweetest of the deadliest. It looked like hell. There were screams and fire all around and within it. Balls of fire were pouring out of it like meteors and shooting stars, and David had no intention to have an encounter right there. He knew he had to literally run without any other mode of transport, and reach the prohibited book, chances were scarce that he would find it, but he had made a quick decision and now was the time to act. The soldiers he had seen leaving at the hall were nowhere to be seen and David guessed they had access to a better way to reach the book.

'Where the hell are you!' he found Semester yelling at him via telepathy.

'Yah, you got it right, it's hell,' David replied, not shutting his eyes, 'And would you leave me alone?'

'Wait-wait wait a moment- and is that HEXAS BEHIND YOU?' she screamed.

'Well, an easy guess I suppose.' David said, 'bye then.'

'What happened?' Semester asked.

David's boss called him too and David finally shut his eyes, 'Yes sir?'

'The book is gone, they took it!' The boss shouted, and David could see him pulling his leftover hair and then he disconnected the call. David opened his eyes.

'What happened I asked!' Semester continued.

'The other book is stolen you idiot!' David shouted, 'Well, I'm sorry. Souls took it.'

As his class got over, Rodge ran towards Semester who waited for him near the playground.

He patted on her head and said, 'How are you?'

'Safe at the moment, how are you?' Semester said, 'by the way, the other prohibited book is stolen too.'

'What have you to do with it?' Rodge aggravated.

'Shut up, don't teach me. I… I don't think higher studies are going to take me to what I want.'

'What do you want?'

'I want to be famous. I want to be… you know…an icon.'

'Well, so what are you thinking? I have no idea.'

'Of course it's confusing, cause I can write, I love singing, I am … you know, intelligent. And pretty too…'

Rodge looked away and then, with a smile meant to disregard Semester's notions, he said, 'We should eat something.'

'In a little time,' Semester replied.

'You want to sing? Just that?' Rodge asked.

'Well, I think…You know! Being a cool official is also not a bad idea,' Semester said, 'being an official does not mean you can not be anything else. You can be more than one thing at a time.'

'Right,' Rodge said, shaking hands with a fellow who looked much shorter.

'Look, you are a kid,' Semester said, 'focus is very important. It's just that all this correlates, baby. After all, what I ultimately want is not to waste this life. There are a countless number of spirits who have been born and have ended unnoticed. Yes these sorts of spirits are important too. Who would a leader lead if they all are leaders? So, I think I will make my way slowly. It can't be decided. How was your class? And how are the other things? Don't you do anything adventurous?'

'Er, I guess nothing like you expect.'

'Well, so it's at least decided that I'm not going for higher expiration.'

'Okay, let's eat something,' Rodge repeated.

'Ya sure fatso.'

CHAPTER 18

UNEXPECTED GIFT

David faced Semester vigilantly, distanced yards away from her. He looked serious now. Semester too shut her eyes and she could dote on her band, and her indigenous magic.

'Think of all you can, there will be no second chance,' David said.

'Ahaan..! Thanks for the kind piece of information sweetheart,' Semester said, 'solemn one.'

'Flirting can further aggravate me,' David said, preparing himself.

'Hey,' Semester said, and David looked into her eyes, she concentrated and gave him a focussed grave look, she hypnotised him. 'Lesson one,' she said, taking her vibes off, 'make correct estimates about the enemy and also act accordingly.'

'Not all have that ability, but okay,' David said and somersaulted a virtual Bacon towards her. Semester stared at it, not expecting the level of the face off to intensify so quickly, she held her band and pacing backwards prepared for a counter attack, but the faster bacon hovered towards her. David stopped it when it was leaning over Semester and just in front of her nose.

Semester blinked and looked at David, than she said, 'You really got me agitated now,' She jumped a step and took off from the floor, flying above David and throwing two consecutive intensive light beams meant to momentarily blind David and directed a stream of fake arrows on him. When she landed back she got hit with a rod at the back and turned. David was standing safe at a distance behind her. He had escaped it all.

Confronting each other more closely, David and Semester held their pink bands and looked firmly into each other's eyes. Pink light stemmed out from both the sides and raced towards each other. David and Semester looked on as they continued propelling the attack towards each other. The lights soon clashed and further brightened the milieu.

The decisive face was now going to be revealed on observing which of the two lights was stronger enough to survive after killing the other. As the intensity of the brightness of the collision waned, David and Semester goggled curiously.

In some time, they saw that a small bead of light was crawling towards Semester, and then got extinguished.

'Look at that,' David said.

'Narrow lead,' Semester replied, revolving her hand and creating a sharp edged disk that boomeranged towards David.

David threw a rod at it, then another, but they whacked on to the disc's circumference and shattered off it. The disc progressed and hit David on his arm, falling towards his neck, before Semester destroyed it. David suffered from an injured hand and a minor cut on his neck.

'Could you be a little more proficient and quicker?' David cursed, wiping off his blue blood on his arm.

'I did it deliberately. You won't even get the time to remorse when the enemies are real,' Semester replied, 'it's high time.'

'Okayyy..' David said, he held his band and shut his eyes for just a moment, then opened them and cast small waves with his hands, meanwhile Semester prepared for her counter attack, by anticipating David was going to create a cyclone. She shut her eyes and muttered something. She bowed down and pushed herself on to her front like she was pushing an invisible wall. David too, continued with his hand craft and at first it looked like a small cyclone, then like a bigger cyclone which revolved, then like a huge cyclone that twirled at an implausible speed, and then it started expelling darts that raced towards Semester.

Semester thrust her hands with greater force, and as she did so a crescent protective shield of sharp white light grew. The darts hit the shield one after the other and at massive haste.

The shield sustained itself for quite a long time as Semester continued to hold on and David continued focussing on his firing cyclone, then three darts made their way through, piercing the cover, and hit Semester on her neck and belly, one missing her narrowly near the face.

'Stop!' she shouted, falling down, her shield immediately dying out as she gave up.

David immediately called off and things went silent.

'A real enemy wouldn't.' David elucidated, 'Don't worry, those were not so harmful.'

Semester got up and searched for any wound or cut, but she had gotten away with only bruises and chaffed skin. The rebounding force of the wall had primarily made her fall down as she gave up on it.

She floated a little higher and wavered her fingers and looked at David, eying her next attack. But as she comprehended from that distance, David fell down.

She paused and looked at him, but he didn't seem to look up.

'Oh, is deceiving another combat trick?' she shouted, but David did not answer.

She floated towards him and landed back. She saw David had got down on his knees and was holding his head.

'Is something wrong?' She asked.

David slowly opened his eyes and looked confusedly at Semester.

'What happened? Headache?' Semester asked.

'No, I was just trying to focus.' David said.

'What do you mean? Does it require so much of it?'

'I saw something,' David said.

'Saw something?' Semester asked, coming closer.

'Yeah...ask Justin if he has also read about the causes of dreaming with conscious mind...'

'Shut up! What has happened to you?!' Semester exclaimed. 'Are you seriously dreaming, and ...with so much of your focus? Are you mentally sound?'

'I was just thinking of recoiling your attack on you when I suddenly saw this dream blurring in front of me and when I shut my eyes, I saw it more clearly.'

'What did you see?'

'I saw that Sir Atz... entered your house, you are there, o course I am there, and Sir Atz looks at us...but that look is so bewildering, and...unusual. What am I watching?'

'You know...' Semester said, sitting down next to him, 'I have no idea...'

'Well...we need to analyse now, our weak points,' David said, getting up, 'we both your room, you are resent too are excellent combaters but may be yet not up to the mark. So while this face off would be very useful...'

'That was all for the blay?' Semester interjected.

'...yeah..'

'...go to... alright, I need to analyse too...'

'We didn't use any shields...it was a good fight.'

'No weaknesses,' Semester said.

'How's your injury now?' David asked.

'Better than your blood spattered shirt,' Semester said.

Calling David like in ages, Justin said, 'You...I need to tell you some bad news...'

'What's worse than you calling me...in times of desperation..' David replied, putting down his mug on the table in an expensive room in his house, 'Though thanks for not dropping into my house, thanks for the call.'

'..you are fired,' Justin said.

'er...are you my new boss?' David pretended to be funny.

'No, I just happened to know this information before your boss himself told you.'

'Fired why?' David grimaced.

'May be I don't know the actual reason, but I heard it's on grounds of failing to abide by your duties sincerely and failing to protect the prohibited book,' Justin sombrely answered.

'So don't tell me all the millions of officials like me in this galaxy are fired too!'

'No I won't tell you that because that has not happened,' Justin replied.

'Heck...enough of enough!' David exclaimed, 'I'm bloody not going to tolerate it like a meek victim.'

Justin remained silent.

'All right, thanks.' David said.

'And...David I wanted to say something else...'

'What else!'

'Well...I won't be able to say if you give me all those expressions and tones.'

'Okay my love, what is the other thing?' David asked, controlling himself.

'Well, as of now, I'd say take care.'

'Thank you.' David said, disconnecting the call. Giving a look at his attire, he decided to fly right then to the Office. 'That's ridiculous! That's a total conspiracy...it is diplomatic and...er political and nothing else...'

As he looked into the mirror and his mind rolled over the issue, he heard a little knock at the door.

He went through to the first room and opened the door, fixing his collar. As he looked up, a ball of frame whooshed inside rasping his shoulder and opened up, it burst into little flames and sparks, making it look like a dummy firework.

'What is it?' David said to the ball that was hidden in the sparks, then turning back to the door he called out, 'Who's there?'

A pause in the little fire noise made him look into the room again, and then he saw that the ball of frame had fallen to the floor while hanging on the aura of his room were little words that read

¡ ¡ ¡You have juzt been fired!!!

David frowned at the words and wiped them off with his hands, 'Go off!', he shouted. He picked up the frame that had fallen down and read it, 'Master David (15), III level officer, Local Office, Flick de Atz, you have been fired from your above service rank on the follwing accounts, failing to execute the dutied assigned to you, failing to set up a proper guidance for your juniors, failing to protect the esteem of your office institution by failing to perform in the infamous prohibited book two stealing incident by ...okay wait I'm going to tell you.' David said, crumbling the frame and throwing it aside. He shut the door back and closed his eyes.

'Where are you going?' he heard a voice from somewhere near the dark doorstep before the next room.

'And who's there! It's my home!' David said, walking forward, and beginning to be careful, all his practice with Semester getting afresh in his mind.

A boy and a girl stepped out of the dark and David read them top to bottom. They had no gleam in their bodies, and as they stepped more forward, David could see their faces looked weak, and dull. He exclaimed, 'Look at you! You're souls! Inside my house!'

'You need to shield the house, we have to talk to you urgently. It's for your benefit. We can't escape if you want to get us arrested, we can't even use the Quixie flier as you call it. So trust us.'

David looked at the boy and the girl with eyes wide open, and then said, 'not only get you arrested, but I will personally make sure that you don't get any ice until you die of its depravation. Hang on hang on, are you in disguise and once I shield myself you will capture me just like Semester was.'

The boy and the girl looked at each other, thinking about what to answer.

'I have just been fired or I would have done a truth test for that,' David sharply said, 'I do have a better option, I will call a friend of mine to hypnotise you and make you tell the truth.'

'Indigenous magic doesn't ever work on us, sir.' The girl said.

'What!' David said, 'Such a shame! And it's strange that you know I have a friend Semester, more so because you know she has that ability of hypnotising. Okay well well, I will shield only you two and not me.'

The girl and the boy exchanged looks again and then the boy said, 'We agree.'

At this, David got anxious and didn't delay anymore to shield the souls from distant observation and records by the officials.

'Now speak, I have more important works,' David alarmingly said.

'We want to give you the prohibited book,' the girl soul said,' we all stole it for you.'

Hearing this, David's strained eye brows gradually relaxed and his narrowed eyes widened with awe, his mouth fell open too and after all this slow motion work, he said, 'What?'

'Yes, but don't panic please. You have not shielded yourself and are still under observation we suppose. And such reactions will draw attention. You will have to shield yourself too before you see it.'

'But why did you do it for me?!'

'Souls don't forget gratitude. We, who feel strange when someone even smiles at us, or simply if someone doesn't diss us, were obliged and touched by your kind behaviour when you presented us with so much ice, and even ignored Joz when he questioned that pleasant behaviour of yours towards us.'

'Really! That's all?' You are...okay wait...Shield me,' David said and oscillated up and down as he waited for the pink shield to cover him up as soon as possible. Then as it was done, he continued, 'You stole the prohibited book, letting hundreds of souls die at the hands of the security army, just because I gave you ice! And and and, you would have torn that book into as many pieces as you all were in total, because once anyone sees a prohibited book, they are attracted to snatch it.'

'Prohibited books' hallucination is just like Miss Semester's indigenous ability to hypnotize. All this doesn't work on us,' the boy explained.

'Oh my oh my hang on! I'm going to get mad now.' David said, falling on the nearest chair, 'Eh...ok...just one question, you really stole it for paying back the debt of the ice?'

'Well yes,' the girl said, 'In fact, we paid you only a small fraction if you see little more carefully, and if you regard our lives with at least some respect.'

'How dare you say such a thing!' David shouted, getting up and advancing to the girl.

'No, no please,' the boy said putting himself in front of the girl.

'Oh look here you are to the rescue. Who's she to you!' David said.

'She's my girlfriend', the boy shyly answered.

'Oh my...where the hell am I...that rhymes...er...' getting back to his chair, David said, 'so you have a world of your own. That's an interesting fact. Have you come here for me to get you married as well?'

'She couldn't let me die alone.' the boy said, sighing, 'Of course we trust you. But yet...we could never trust a spirit completely.'

'Cool...' David said, 'now talk business. Continue answering my question, with the right attitude and words.'

'She was right Master David,' the boy said, 'She said nothing wrong. Ice is life to us. You save a couple of hundreds of lives that blay by giving us ice. And we are only saving you and Miss Semester from possible hardships or...may be even your lives. So we are not doing much in return, only unless our lives deserve no deal of respect to you, which we know they don't... That's what she was trying to tell you; just sounded otherwise.'

David partly heard this as his mind was running faster and on much broader range of issues.

'Who told you I need the book, and how do you know we are in danger?' he threw out a question.

'Spirits can deprive us of many things but yet certain things like big news do fall into our ears, ye know, we after all live in the same universe,' the boy said, 'that's all I will say.'

'I guess this is the first time that souls have dared to stand in front of spirits,' David said, 'let alone trying to steal one of the most precious of their heritage. Why?'

'You are right...It's all about change. Because it's a new cycle of the universe.' The boy looked directly into David's eyes and said.

'...how do you know that, what's going on!' David said as he held his head.

'I think it's time to hand you over the book,' the girl said.

'Oh yeah,' David said.

'Take it out,' the boy said to the girl, 'I have tucked it on the backside of my waist.'

The girl made a face at the boy, and then stepped behind him. 'Master David, kindly allow us to move towards the door as we suppose to have fulfilled our duty,' the boy humbly said.

'You will give me the book, right' David asked, giving way to the two souls to make their way to the main door. 'Although this idea of getting such a thing without hard work looks a little cheap to me.'

'No one can ever make it with only hard work and abilities, and with no luck,' the boy said, walking slowly with his girlfriend.

David could see the girl holding supposedly the book that was covered in an unattractive wrapping.

As the two souls reached the door, they turned to David and then the girl handed over the book to David, who felt it was a legendary moment, and was as conscious as he could be.

The boy opened the door and said, 'we never required you to shield us. Souls can't be seen officially on videos since they have no magical aura or ...field around them, it was just to see if you know this fact, and to build up your faith on some basis. We are sorry, but we hope you didn't mind.'

With this, the two souls gazed out to make sure no one was present to see them coming out of a spirit's house, and then they bowed to David and stepped out, shutting carefully the door behind them.

CHAPTER 19

SIR ATZ...

This time, David's mother and father were fully supportive of him; as they too realised that it was a clearly unfair decision to fire David.

'A suspension for sometime could still, still be tolerated *somehow*,' Jonas said, 'what are you going for now? And what do you suggest, Miss Venaiah?'

(Now before your Earthian mind thinks she's now single, let me tell you there is nothing like Mrs over here because the spirits are not sexist at all, although that might be a thing you might have never imagined to be reflecting prejudice).

Venaiah, David's mother, is done no injustice by being talked about so late. She was a beautiful woman, who was extremely introverted and reserved. She was hardly found mingling with anyone outside the home, and quite the same inside the home as well. This resulted in confining her to the house. She spent her time reading, listening to music, thinking, but not writing, singing, or speaking, all of which implies she had acquired immense knowledge, but lacked in the willingness to express. This behaviour was very easily called "anomalous", but since she did not share, it was difficult to figure out a solution. It was her nature, and her eccentricity seemed to get sluggishly aggravated.

Anyway, she replied to Jonas, 'If he finds it suitable to complain, he should. But I suppose he doesn't have the possibility of doing much about it. It's done.'

'Okay...I don't know when I will be able to tell you both certain things...' David said, reaching to thoughts of other phases of his life, like Paradis, Prohibited book which he owned now, and an enemy who for some reason wanted him badly...

Jonas didn't reply, and obviously, Viniah too didn't.

'Well...' David said, getting up, 'I hope I'll sometime be able to tell you. You know. Available to ... okay, see you.'

'Now where are you going?' Jonas asked.

'To Semester, got rocking news to tell,' David answered.

'Are you going to use that word for your being fired?' Jonas asked.

'Em...yes. Not exactly,' David said.

Semester, who had been informed by David by a shielded conversation, that what they had been craving for had fallen straight into their lap, was eagerly waiting to welcome David at her home.

'Coming!' she said, getting up quickly to open the door. 'Oh, mumma...' she saw Rose standing at the door instead of David. Then David appeared just next to her mother, holding a heavy but dirtily wrapped something. She knew it was the Book.

'Oh hello, David,' Rose said, 'How are you, come, come inside. How are you?'

All the three entered the room and David-Semester stole looks at each other.

'Early leave toblay?' Semester asked Miss Rose.

'Yes, some orientation was supposed to be held, and I had been assigned no charge.' Rose answered, 'so such experators went home.'

'I see, tired?' Semester asked.

'No no I'm fine,' Rose replied, 'David, you didn't answer me how you are.'

'I'm fine Aunt Rose,' David said, 'and, and...jut that I got fired ... last blay.'

'Oh yes, Semester told me that,' Rose said, 'I was deliberately refraining from talking about it so early.'

'It's actually surprising because I'm the only Official who has been ousted,' David said, 'it can't be only what it looks, it's a complete conspiracy. Either my colleagues were jealous, or...something else, no Semester?'

'Yes,' Semester said, 'and who gives the order of firing an official?'

'A pretty senior Official,' Rose answered, 'what are you doing about it?'

'Trying to get down to the roots of it,' David said, 'as I can smell something.'

'Spirituality is losing its meaning,' Rose said, looking extremely indulgent and sensitive to David's problem. 'These diplomats have no shame.'

'Mumma he has something to tell me,' Semester said, 'can we go to my room? And I want to get my own house now, as soon as I get into some awesome work.'

'By the way,' Rose said, 'Laurins has been dispatched an open warning to present himself before the Officials and surrender, otherwise his legal execution is on the run. He will be ended.'

Semester sighed and looked at David not sure how to react.

David got up and stood behind Semester ready to go to her room. Rose didn't say anything and arranged her bag and documents on one of her eight tables that she exclusively owned in the house.

Semester slipped quietly into her room, knowing that her mother did not like secrets between Semester and David.

'I know you must be thinking the same,' Semester said, shutting the door, 'Is what you saw a reality...is Sir Atz really behind this?'

'Yes I am wondering about the same,' David said, 'dating back to as far as possible, he might have seen certain things in my mind while performing the truth test on me after I rescued you, he might have even been the reason why I was not appointed as a very senior Official, which I doubtlessly deserved, he might have told Sir Laurins to steal the Prohibited book, he might have got me fired, and he might therefore be a Zolahart's man, because he has told us not to tell anyone, not even our parents, that Zolahart is alive.'

Semester stood at the door, supporting herself against it, 'Stupid, you should have shielded before you said all this.'

'I don't care,' David said, 'He's not my boss now. And I'm saying what I feel...in fact what is right.'

'Hmm. Why are we doing this. Why do we have to do this?' Semester said.

'Can't you already see?' David asked.

'Hmm. It's time, then.'

'It's time.'

David himself had not opened or even uncovered the Prohibited book from under its dirty wrap. He detailed Semester on how he got the book, 'We are still enjoying the benefits of what Sir Paradis did for us. The souls put their lives at stake, because He, while looking like me, saved their lives.'

Semester nodded.

'Hey!' David said to Semester, 'The boy told me that your hypnotism could have no effect on them.'

'Really? Why so?'

'He later said that they couldn't even feel any attraction on seeing the Prohibited book and that your ability to hypnotize was a similar power. He said the souls couldn't even be seen by the Officials on videos and hence had no need of shields. All this was because they had no magical aura. So what do you understand?'

'That's interesting,' Semester said, 'what I understand is that they have no magical vibes and nor does their conscience have them. So I have nothing left to hypnotize!'

'Exactly,' David said, carefully placing in front of his lap the book that he was carrying. 'We want to use this book, not exploit it, is that right?'

'Right,' Semester said.

'So I am going to leave the book here, without looking at it,' David said.

'What?' Semester questioned before David could complete.

'I don't know if it's in your knowledge or not, but similar auras do cancel each other out, be that partially or completely. Read only what is necessary, because you can do so. Hypnotize the book, and it will hypnotize back, canceling the effect, hopefully. And remember to make the correct use of it. Do tell me how it is.' David said, winking.

'Are you serious?' Semester asked. 'We got it because of you. And it's such a legendary book, it's a complete thesaurus of the whole Universe, and you won't even look at it?'

'We needed it on purpose,' David said, smiling, 'and hey, I might want to look at it some other time. So don't make it a final decision that I'm not, okay? And anyway, I think you are feeling betrayed 'cause you have to read what is expected to be old fashioned royal style of writing and figure out the meaning, and mind you, that book is heavy too, so all the best.'

'I have a better idea,' Semester said, smiling, 'sit here behind me, and as I read out what's written, help me out with the meaning.'

'Well, it's a great grand book,' David said, 'and not a toy.'

With that careful opening and shutting of the door, David left a great deal to Semester.'

CHAPTER 20

CONSCIOUSNESS VERSUS CONSCIOUSNESS

Gazing at the wrapped book, readying to battle its consciousness, Semester was striving to focus through her nervousness. Her mind had sensible questions like *what could be so sensational in the book that it had been preserved since the beginning of the universe*; and nonsensical ones like *what if the souls had made a fool of David.* Her mind was as focused as possible, chucking off all disturbances.

Not being as honest as David, she found it easier to be so after David's recommendation of the proper use of the book. She made herself determined not to misuse the book and slowly removed a fold of the wrap, and her nervousness was graving. She did not look away from the book. Inspecting her focus, she removed almost the entire wrap, and the book was exposed. Semester's mind felt an extraordinary disturbance in her focus, and she held on to hypnotizing the book, hoping that the book wouldn't dominate her.

As she uncovered all of it, Semester took time to have a look at the rugged hard cover of the momentous book. She recalled that the book had accidentally been torn apart and this cover would have later been bonded to the book.

Keeping her focus unmoved, Semester uncovered the entire book. In the realization of the glory of the moment, she took a deep breath and stared at the splendid old book; a shiver ran through her body. She noticed that her behavior did not look as severely inclined by any attractive force as she imagined one would feel while looking at a prohibited book; and she thought, 'David was right! I am countering the consciousness of the book!'

Although she felt it would not be right to say that she felt no disturbances at all, the book was definitely trying to overpower her, as if searching for a moment's opportunity for Semester's focus to loosen off. Realizing these possible crises, Semester kept her attention concentrated on hypnotizing the book, but was not able to keep her hands off it for long. Certainly, her power was outsmarted by the book's. As she turned over the hard cover, she found that the pages of the book were all old and withered golden ones, quite similar to the one that Paradis had sent as a clue for meeting her and David for the first time. The first page though had an abrupt beginning, giving the impression that the book Semester was reading was the second torn half of what was originally a single piece book. Semester could feel the vibes of the book drawing and magnetizing her, and she considered shutting her eyes, but didn't. 'It will be very difficult to hypnotize the book again once I lose the eye contact for a prolonged time. So I better focus more,' she said to herself, 'I just need to read the broad titles first of all, if there are any titles.'

Roughly running her eyes through the paragraphs, Semester got an impression that the book was indeed written in old fashioned language and it might be tricky to figure things out. She felt as if each and every word was talking to her, spellbinding her to read it, but she looked firmly and determinedly into the book, focusing not to loose her determination. Reading a word or two extra than she intended to, because of the book's overriding attraction, Semester turned to the next page.

Taking a break from reading, she recalled what she read, 'there was an extensive use of the word "destruction", so is it that this . . .' before she could think any further, she had begun to read on the next page. Turning a dozen pages, she landed up at:

Imperzonating perzona(z)

Now that was a title.

Semester's eyes widened as she felt a frisson run over. Trying her best not to read a single next word, she turned the page quickly, then again and again, and then a sub heading there she saw:

Exchanging perzona(z)

And she turned the frame quickly again, accidentally tearing the withered golden page a little while doing so. She thought, 'What are you doing! It's such a legendary book!'

There she read the next title,

Owning ze Hexaz

Part of her mind involved in reading and fear, Semester was unable to refrain herself from reading further this time, "*Ze Baconz own ze Hexas, and zem thee need to own hence.*"

Semester turned the frames again a few times getting nervous, and then there was another title,

Past and future; travel, alteration.

Petrified by the title, she turned the page quickly, reading random words that could convey no meaning where complete sentences seemed confusing.

The soul mitigation

'What?' Semester thought, and that absolutely failed her in avoiding it, she read, 'For once it will happen in time, that the souls will have to be freed of the castigation, the need of ice, and the pain of their warm, dull physique . . . Ooooh, turn!' Semester turned the page, taking a break from reading to re-establish her focus on the book. She turned a few pages again and then reached another.

Creating alter egos

. . . multiplying yourself implies creation of falze zpirits zat have each and every capability, memory, feelingz and trait zat you do, but are not considered living. Thou . . .

'It's overpowering!' Semester said, 'All I have read are headlines, and it was so difficult,' she thought.' but as she saw that there were just around twenty more frames to go, she flipped over. At the last frame, which she expected to tell something, was blank, and she began flipping back again.

CHAPTER 21

THE CONFESSION

David had received a telepathic call from a government office; and it looked like there was blackmailing going on; from both the sides.

'. . . that you were an employee.' The caller, a typical young man, said to David, 'and Sir Atz might be furious about coming across such a complaint against being fired, fired due to your own shortcomings. And after all, who are you complaining to? At the end, they are those same Officials who have already discussed and held meetings and ultimately decided.'

'Oh no no. That in no way means I have lost all my judgemental abilities, sir,' David said, 'if I can really have something conveyed to Sir Atz, can it be this—I think it will be safe, in fact safer to let everyone know now on whose orders Semester had been kidnapped.'

'Your complaint is going to get your and our time wasted,' the caller said, 'that was all to inform you.'

'David!' Semester entered his room excitedly.

'Thank you sir,' David said, signalling Semester to have a seat, 'but I don't even feel this conversation was virtuous because I am genuinely having a problem and would not step back from the complaint.'

'I see,' the caller said, 'you're welcome.'

'So, how have you been?' David asked Semester.

Semester smiled mischievously at David while giving him a sharp look.

'I see,' David said.

'Practice sessions begin today!' Semester exclaimed, putting her hands up happily.

'That means it was useful?' David asked.

'Not directly . . .' Semester answered, 'I mean you shouldn't expect to sit back and watch things happen, it's you who's now got better ideas to help yourself.'

David pursed his lips and said, 'that means our destiny has yet not started to be kind to us?'

'Right,' Semester said, 'are you afraid of working hard to achieve? Well honestly, I'm a little.'

'No, I'm not,' David said.

The conversation was interrupted with a knock at the door.

'Yes, who's there?' David called out.

Enter Justin, 'it's me.'

'Justin!' Semester leaped from the fibre couch and hugged Justin, 'hi! How are you!?'

'I'm fine,' Justin said, smiling finally, though only for few abrupt moments. He looked at David, who, of course was not going to be the first one to lend a welcoming hand.

'Hello,' Justin said, putting forth his hand.

David got up and shook hands, and then the two friends hugged. Those were touching moments . . .

'Missed you . . .' Semester said, posing an emotional smile.

'Yeah . . . er . . .' Justin mumbled.

'So, what's up?' David asked, not still looking perfectly comfortable, but definitely keen to be; and happy.

'Don't smile at me, either of you,' Justin said, looking very serious and fragile.

'Well, okay . . .' Semester said, and then in a serious and manly voice she intoned, 'What's up?'

Justin remained silent.

'All's well that ends well,' David said smiling, 'Now there's no problem.'

'There was . . . I was the problem,' Justin said.

'No hang on, is he . . . is he in tears oh my god!' Semester droned.

'Wait wait . . .' Justin spoke, his eyes actually very moist, making it a big event. 'This has been very tough . . . and I told you David . . .

that I had something to tell you . . . I fell so low in jealous for you, and hatred for your abnormal and carefree and senseless behaviour . . . that I . . .'

'I what?' David said, 'It's all okay, dude.'

Justin looked up, and his body language suggested considerable odds. He said, 'My . . . my brute died out that blay I pushed Romella, in Laurins Office, and she fell down, and looked at me . . . Sir Atz is a culprit David, I knew it since I have been spying on Laurins and even you and Semester. The blay Semester first saw me in the Office while you were about to be questioned for a stolen prohibited book, i knew you wanted thebooks, and I wanted you to never get them.' ·

'Give me a break!' David roared, getting up, Semester got up, too. 'Were you that stranger wrapped wholly in shrouds?'

Justin continued breathing heavily, and replied, 'yes . . .'

'You filthy bastard,' David sprang on to Justin and held him by his collar, 'how dare you be such a big traitor, I thought you were sane,' David shouted.

Semester side-lined David and clutched Justin's shoulder, looking fiercely into his eyes, looking ready to attack.

'What are you doing?' David said, desisting Semester from starting a war.

Summarily, half a dozen men and women arrived at David's room.

'What's going on?' David questioned.

The men and women, all wearing black well fitting and equipped outfits, and before anyone could realise they were from the Hexas Department, Justin was well under their grip.

'I would personally hand over this deserter to the Officials,' Semester said, 'but is this how you break into others' house to do your job?'

'Are they going to take him to Hexas?' David asked.

A man, came forward, and stood right in front of David and Semester. It looked like he would chafe them to dust.

'He accepted being an aid in a crime,' the man said, sounding like there was thundering around the house, his voice immediately bringing all in the room to motionlessness. 'Additionally, he accused the Head of a galaxy. Let the verdicts be given.'

'Say sorry to Romella,' Justin articulated, and his eyes seemed to be full of guilt and hopelessness.

The next moment, David and Semester were left alone in the room.

'What just happened?' David blankly asked Semester, falling back on his chair.

Semester, still very restless, angry and energetic, replied, 'I came to tell you great things, Justin came and met us after blays and told us an even greater thing, five officials from the Hexas department broke into your house, nearly stupefying us and took Justin away.'

'You missed the even more important part,' David said, looking s little exhausted, 'be practical.'

'He said he pushed Romella and that Sir Atz and Laurins were culprits,' Semester added.

'Yes, that part,' David said, 'now you will continue with what you came here to tell me.'

'Justin could have shielded himself,' Semester said, 'the Officials would then not come to know about him playing any sort of role in the offence.'

'I don't know or care,' David said, 'but if he really knows some truths, he did just the right by getting arrsted for interrogation. And now, you will tell me about you know what.'

'Now?' Semester said.

'There's no such siren to tell you—it's high time.'

Semester gazed at David, looking peaceful, but she was not.

'Alright,' Semester said.

Shielded and ready, David and Semester began discussing the prohibited book.

'I felt very little attraction from the book, so that part went good; that was the first thing,' Semester began. 'The book we have is the second torn half. The writing is old fashioned. The first title is incomplete, that is to say, half contained in the other stolen book, and half here. Sorry to say, if that other half of the book that was stolen a slout ago is in the wrong hands, the whole universe would anytime come to an end, because that is what that first title was.'

'What do you mean!' David bellowed, 'If it takes that long to use the magic taught in the book, how can we so quickly apply all that you read?'

'Depends upon topic to topic,' Semester said, 'there are certain things that might take a long time of spiritual evolution and power to acquire few of the powers stated. Others, might be accomplished sooner.'

'Alright,' David said, 'so this universe destruction recipe takes time?'

'Yes, looks like,' Semester answered, 'However, the remnant of this destruction lesson had a subtitle which I read.'

'What's that?'

'Smaller destructions,' Semester told, 'Matter can neither be created nor destroyed, right? Only changes from one form to another? But no, this destruction that is being talked about in the book, swaps every single particle into nothing.'

'You read it?'

'Yes, i read relevant topics like Destruction, impersonating or exchanging personas, and before I could decide on whether to read about creating alter-egos, I had read it, a little overcome by the book, you know.'

'What were the irrelavant topics!?' David asked, little suspicious of Semester's wit.

'Like owning the Hexas, Soul mitigation and, didn't read past or future travel and alteration as it sounded too dangerous to me.'

'Alright,' David said, 'holding his own chin, 'what I am thinking is, what if the other book has been in the wrong hands for as long as it shouldn't be. I'm afraid, now I realise if the book teaches you how about to destroy the whole universe, the matter is being taken as a joke. The book should be safe!'

'For that, we can't expect the help of the government.' Semester said, 'Shall we start now?'

'Yes, but, do you remember everything?' David asked.

'Nope,' Semester replied, pulling out a few loose frames out of her small read bag.

'You-have-made-notes-out-of-the-book!!?' David appallingly exclaimed.

Semester flaunted the silver papers in front of David's eyes and smiled, 'when will miss Semester Forthe Visinus's code language be of a use?'

CHAPTER 22

✦
✦ ✦
✦ ✦

ALTER EGOS

Romella said a small "what?" and then quieted down, looking perplexed on being told that it was Justin who had pushed her away from stopping Laurins.

'We understand.' David said, 'see how without a clue the spirituality gets dumped.'

'Don't talk about that bloody loser in front of me,' Semester's anger quickly revived, as usual, 'aa . . . . uhhh, don't!'

'Okay, Romi, Sim and me have some work,' David said, 'you know what . . .'

'Wait,' Romella said, as she handed over an infolet to Semester, 'have a look.'

'What's new?' Semester mumbled, as David too peeked in.

'Second frame.' Romella instructed.

Semester turned to the second frame and her eyes caught the relevant news.

As David and Semester went through it, Romella said, 'How will they recover the Prohibited book if they end Laurins?'

'Blimey!' Semester said, 'you're right, I hardly had that idea.'

'Me too, didn't think of it,' David said, 'May be they're just trying to threaten him.'

'But it says the voting has begun!' Semester interjected, 'within half a blay, more than three hundred heads took time from their Offices, presented themselves at the Senate and signed the petition to kill Laurins.'

'If it is really so,' David said, 'they're even more foolish than Romella is. Their motive is to ensure the safety of the Book, but what they're doing is not a step towards doing so. But, do you think they are that foolish? Nope. The truth is hidden, and all this Laurins ending process has other motives.

'Bloody international conspiracy!' Semester's mind finally started to work, 'by the way, do you mean they simply don't want the book to be ever recovered?'

David shrugged; and Romella kept looking on.

Anyway, David, let's hurry,' Semester said, dropping the infolet on the table and pulling David, 'See ya Romi.'

Within the Quixie flier itself, the preparation had begun. David pulled his sleeve, Semester tied up her beautiful lustrous hair, and they had shielded themselves by the time they entered her room.

'Did you get what I told you till now?' Semester asked.

'Yeah, we are going to first of all learn—?'

'Multiplying ourselves.' Semester promptly replied.

'Excellent,' David said, 'That would mean more Davids and Semesters, more power, the more we further learn, the more harm we and our alter egos impose. Are there any chants involved?'

'Yes, a couple of them, for certain tasks, lemme check,' Semester replied, opening her diary.

'That's a new diary.' David noticed.

'Yeah, while I was kidnapped my old one was taken into custody and was returned to mom, along with other things, a little later. In the meantime I wrote down my experience in this, that's how this diary starts. And I've been using this one since then.'

'Alright,' David said, sitting by Semester and looking at the diary. 'Being Again—that's a cool title. But why did you not write this entry in your code language?'

'When emotions come too fast, it's more comfortable and natural to write normal,' Semester said, turning finally to what she had copied from the Prohibited book. David looked on as she slowly decoded the words.

'Well no, not chants really; not for alter egos,' Semester told.

'Alright,' David said, and Semester continued to read.

After she hurriedly finished, she said, 'okay I think you know, that you can't display your alter egos to anyone just like that, it has to be secretly done.'

'Of course!' David said, 'that's why we are here, shielded and in your room.'

'Okay,' Semester continued, 'the number of times you successfully repeat the process, the number of your replicas you create. Each replica knows who the real you is.'

'That's cool, but, if I create four Davids, would you be able to figure out who the real one is?'

'I'm afraid, no.' Semester answered.

'Oh my God,' David said, 'that's not too good. Let's begin.'

'It says that it takes a lot of energy for such creations,' Semester began, 'because all the alter egos you create are not spirits, but energies, in fact equivalent energies. We have to channel this energy loss such that we ourselves don't get too weak.'

'And how are we going to do that?'

'Certain things can't alas, be taught!'

'Humm . . . Continue.'

'You don't even need to shut your eyes in case you can completely focus that way,' Semester explained, 'but focusing is very important. You are creating an extremely complicated energy that has to appear, behave and think in a very precise and constrained manner. You have to lift yourself up a little, float up, and try to concentrate your energy to the center of your head, using your hands!'

'Got it,' David said.

All through this, you have to think of nothing else but what you are doing. But mind virtually travels faster than light, and if there is any external disturbance going on, you might not be able to think solely about the task.'

'Then?'

'There is an aid to help achieve superior concentration,' Semester said. 'The unaltered state of the brain as Sir Paradis as called it. Probably because it rhymes with the word alter ego,' Semester added, laughing.

'Carry on,' David said.'

'When you are in that state, you are no more aware of the outside world. It is dangerous because creating your copies takes time, and in the meantime, your enemy is free to do anything to you while tuning into their favorite song.'

The incredibly single piece diamond cut structure, externally jeweled with platinum and white sapphires, the Senate, the residence of the Master of the Universe, continued to eternally twinkle its splendid beauty.

On the inside of this unbeatable home, Sir Omen, the deserving and lucky master, was still not tired of admiring its even more colorfully enriched body.

His shoulders were firmly upright and did not look overburdened by the complete responsibility and answerability of the whole of the universe.

His had royal attire, and a serene face. His dark eyes reflected love and wisdom, and he perfectly maintained the dignity of his position.

His intelligence, though, again was suddenly reminded of the case he had been finding potentially problematic.

'Subroto,' he calmly said.

Subroto, his chief attendant instantly ran in, 'master', he bowed to Sir Omen and said.

I would like you to update me on the Laurins-Justin-Atz triangle, and also arrange for a meeting with my Advisor as soon as possible.'

'Master,' Subroto said, 'Master Justin reasserts that he learnt that Sir Laurins and Sir Atz were involved in certain unlawful and immoral activity, and that they both might well have a connection with the theft of both the Prohibited books. Sir Atz has yet not been officially convicted. Thought he truth test of Master Justin revealed no forgery. What is taking place at the fastest pace are the efforts to convict Master Justin on *evidently* having participated in the escape of Sir Laurins.'

'You may leave, Subroto,' Sir Omen said.

CHAPTER 23

THE UNTIDY MAN

The untidy man

Daily life in Plaryzomes had become quite messed up owing to the absence of a Chief Experator. The pride of Plaryzomes as being the stainlessly and doubtlessly reigning institute was being stained and doubted. Though not a single student had switched out of the institute, a few had taken temporary leave and gone to their homes. The experators had started doing each and every possible tactic to replace the empty chief's post. Romella, an exception in this race, was still sticking to her choice of teaching "Eons of History".

'Rodge, Rodge!' she called as she saw him running at a great momentum along with his friends. Rodge was too busy and loud to listen to Romella's already sweetly shrill calls.

Romella had to run after him and hold him and that was when Rodge finally noticed her, 'why are you not listening!' she asked.

'Hi, what happened?' Rodge answered, still very much into his sporty mood.

'I thought you'd be the first to run home when there are no studies going on,' Romella said.

'I would be the first to run home when there's no playing going on,' Rodge corrected her.

'Alright, but you should be at home,' Romella said, 'I couldn't say this to either David or Semester, but they're cooking something, and I'm worried. Justin is already . . . .'

144

'I didn't like him since the very begging,' Rodge meted out a quick verdict.

Romella paused for a moment and then said, 'I know what he did was cheap, but, Hexas? Shut up.'

'There's no other thing where criminals are sent. My friends are waiting. What did you stop me for?' Rodge asked.

'Hey Rodge what are you doing!', a friend shouted from a distance and another pulled him and whispered something into his ears, after which both of them ran away.

'He didn't know you are an experator,' Rodge said, laughing.

'I've been here for so long. That kid must be ignorant and lazy,' Romella said, 'anyway, I am serious Rodge. I know you care for Sim more than I do. So, just keep an eye on her and don't run here and there foolishly.'

'I got you,' Rodge said, 'I'll tell mom and dad too.'

'Only if Semester or David get no clue that there is serious spying going on,' Romella said.

'Bye,' Rodge said, having had run a few meters away already.

'But you . . .' Romella said; then she turned and resumed her lonely walk.

The following two blays, David and Semester were still practicing, Rodge had moved in to his home, informed his mom and dad who in turn informed David's, Romella was still lonely, Justin was even more critically endangered, and the votes for ending Sir Laurins had reached the near-terminating nine hundred seventy eight.

Tired of the duo's daily secret meeting in Semester's room, Rose finally sounded rude, 'I warn you if I feel there is any suspicious activity going on, I will bring any meeting of you two to an end.'

'What are you saying mumma, be silent!' Semester declared.

'I'm not joking,' Rose said, moving to her room having introduced her final decision. Rodge kept looking on with an expressionless face, his hands passionately folded.

'She's been behaving little oddly since last blay,' Semester said, 'I even felt she and dad were talking something about it. And this,' Semester said, pointing angrily at Rodge by looking severely at him, 'is a different set of problems.'

'Come on in,' Semester said, and David followed her.

After they had shut the door of Semester's room, David said, 'I could only make a tiny and lifeless David, and you, well you couldn't create anything at all! We have been practicing so hard!'

'But we did at least exchange personalities,' Semester said.

'Well, yes, that was perfect, but useless! When we both will be facing Zolahart, whether it is us looking like ourselves or looking like each other, who cares!?'

'But,' Semester said, 'we did improve in skills.'

'No doubt,' David said, as he did a hi-five with Semester.

Then, turning serious again, he said, 'the most useful could be destruction. Is there really no way by which we can try destroying something?'

'You mean things like a table?'

Semester sarcastically asked.

'Yes!' David said, 'why not? It's better than discovering that you can't destroy when you urgently need to!'

'Not in my house please' Semester said.

'Of course, we'll go out!'

'. . . . alright,' Semester said.

'Great,' David said, 'now start.'

Both David and Semester stood next to each other at a few distance.

'Since you realise that exchanging persona is not very useful, I am trying to imitate someone else's,' Semester said.

'This book is simply not meant for you,' David said, mocking her focus, 'all you can ever do is getting agitated and attack.'

Semester looked at David and then, ignoring him, continued with her task. She turned away from David and shut her eyes. She had at least learnt all the chants required and she had to insert the blanks with the name of the spirit whom she wanted to impersonate.

As she began the chanting, she began to glow, her body got warmer, she was very well focussed given her restless nature, but it was hampered by a knock on her shoulders.

It took a few seconds for her to come out of her state, and she found David was standing next to her, 'what! Couldn't you wait? Why are you disturbing my concentration?'

'Who's the real me?' a voice came from the behind, as Semester turned, she saw another David standing there.

'I did it,' David grinned.

Semester accompanied Peter, Rose and Rodge to the ceremony of the appointment of a new Chief Experator of Plaryzomes. Rodge was supposed to stay at Plaryzomes again, and so were the other learners who had also reached with their respective families.

The Plaryplayground had an abundance of spirits but yet it was less noisy than a usual blay when students zoomed in all directions.

The Plaryplayground looked like a new place everytime it was a venue to some event. This time, it looked like a very official venue, much of the space was covered by seating arrangement. Apart from the bottom-most chairs, all others were systematically floating above them, looking like unsupported storeys of a building. Beautiful carpet was laid on its otherwise invisible ground.

Peter was the one to ask, 'Is this place okay?'

'A little behind,' Rose said, pointing to the other chair.

'Alright,' Peter said, and all the four got seated. As expected, Rodge got up within a few moments, 'I'll just be back.'

No one replied because it did not really matter whether he was allowed or not.

When a not very tidy and active man, who was hiding his face under a hood (as if he possessed a very pretty one that prone to jealousy), arrived and seated next to Semester, she made a face; even more so, when he asked her, 'So, how is it going?'

'. . . *fine* . . .' Semester said, looking like "please don't talk to me again because I hate you" mixed with a smile that meant "it was not entertaining and only I know what it takes to force this smile."

'I will help you read it,' the man whispered in his heavy voice.

'The-what?' Semester said, giving another set of sarcastic expressions.

'You know-' the man said, winking.

Getting suspicious, Semester looked at the man first, then carefully checked out her mom and dad who had until now not noticing the conversation.

'I-don't know,' Semester said, 'don't trouble me, please.'

'You will fare much better if you perform the best,' the man said, 'I know you have it.'

Semester was utterly surprised now. 'Meet me later,' she said.

CHAPTER 24

THE COMPLAINT

The weird old man had told Semester to see him at his weird old house.

'He is not ordinary,' Semester said, 'he was the Chief Guest at the Plaryzomes ceremony for the appointment of the new Chief Experator. I wasn't really nice to him as he looked like he was unnecessarily poking me with so many questions, but then when he met me after the ceremony was over, I was like . . . . Romella.'

'Are you sure you are not putting yourself again into danger?' David asked, steps away from entering the dungeon-looking house, 'taking me along this time?'

'Well, never really thought of it,' Semester said.

'Well doesn't really matter,' David said, 'we are shielded this time; and are stronger.'

'Shhh . . .'

As they entered the dome like house, they saw that it looked like no one had the time to clean it up or arrange it, though it didn't have anything perverted or senseless about it.

The man appeared at a door near the right half of that first room.

'This is not real . . . .' David said.

Semester gave a horrified look at this infamous reaction made by David and said, 'Who is heee!!??'

'That's . . . Master Lacranxe. You don't know him?' David surprisingly said.

'Looks like she had no interest in knowing who that Chief Guest was,' Sir Lacranxe said, smiling.

This was one moment when Semester was so guilty of her unawareness that she felt a lightening bolt had fallen right at her head. 'I could not see his whole face; and by the way I have heard his name,' she mumbled.

Not listening to this, David approached Master Lacranxe and duly greeted him by respectfully holding his right hand with both of his own hands. Semester followed too and bowed doing a "namaste", her eyes glued to Master Lacranxe's face, she said, 'I have seen him, Sir, your face is a little changed now.'

'Now be silent,' David said, 'it was so silly on your part that you couldn't recognize the Advisor of . . . . er . . .' David hesitated to continue.

'Zolahart,' Master Lacranxe completed for David, 'though she might have not recognized me because after I quit being his advisor, there was Master Simpson who had replaced me.'

'Do you know Master Simpson?'' David asked.

'Yes I know!' Semester promptly answered.

'Sir, how did you know we have the . . . er . . .' David hesitated again.

'The prohibited book,' Master Lacranxe completed David's sentence once again, 'don't worry my house is definitely extremely safe to talk anything.' Master Lacranxe be-seated himself on a chair and asked David and Semester to do the same.

By now, the dirty and messed up house was a "classy and exclusive, just mistreated" one.

'I am that only other one alive spirit who knows that Sir Paradis is still looking over the Universe that he created,'
Master Lacranxe said.

David and Semester exchanged nervous looks (recalling that the secret of Paradis' eternity had been long ago disclosed to Justin and Romella)

'After today's practice, the first thing you both will do will be to tell the independent investigation body, that Zolahart is alive.

I repeat in other words, do not go an Office that falls under a galactic government.'

David and Semester non-argumentatively nodded.

'Advisors are generally those who work good with the mind; not necessarily physically', Master Lacranxe continued, 'and magic in the prohibited book, I guess, requires more of mental power than physical. Now get up, both of you, let us see what you have learnt till now.'

'We are sorry sir,' David said, 'but that would mean we are uncovering the Prohibited book itself; to you.'

Sir Lacranxe blinked a few times, and then smiled a little, 'Not bad, but can you comment smarter?'

'Er . . . .'

'Could the skills of the prohibited book be imitated through observation, every time anyone that knew them tried them on anyone else, they would get revealed. But in reality, no one would even guess what you are doing is something you have learnt from those exalted books.' Sir Lacranxe said, 'Young fellas, I hope you know better how many frames and tactics there shall be involved in performing anything directed in the book. Observation can not decode the procedure involved. Moreover, as a piece of information, let me tell you, anyone who haven't' personally seen the book, can not perform any of its prohibited skills.'

Semester turned to David in slow motion and said to him, 'liar! You have seen the book and you pretended you are such a courteous swail . . . . you Justin part two!'

'I swear I didn't see it!' David defended.

'He might be telling the truth, Semester,' Master Lacranxe said.

'But he could do the magic mentioned in the book,' Semester said, 'you said no one could do it if they hadn't seen wither of the books.'

'David is an exception,' Master Lacranxe said.

'Exception?' David asked.

'Yes, exception,' Master Lacranxe said, 'and all that I just mentioned about copying the prohibited magic is unimportant. You might still be uncomfortable because I will at least come to know about the contents of the book, which range from impersonating someone to creating your alter egos.'

'You know all this!?' Semester said, aghast.

'A little more my honest friends,' Master Lacranxe said, 'the contents of the other half of the prohibited book are Mastering magic, eternity, ending the spirits.'

'That means Zolahart is eternal?' David and Semester said together.

'Yes. He is eternal because he has or had the book, no idea,' Master Lacranxe said. 'And the topic at the end of the book he has, only half of which lies at the beginning of the second torn half of the book-'

'Destruction?' Semester asked.

'Yes, destruction,' Master Lacranxe said, 'deserves the most attention because it starts with "destroying the whole Universe at once".'

'What!' David and Semester reacted together.

'That is the most difficult part, though.' Master Lacranxe said, 'one might get self-destructed, one might be left as the only thing in the Universe without any space to survive, one might be a ruler with nothing left to rule over and so on.'

'And ending spirits . . . just like the Officials do?' David asked.

'Really think so,' Master Lacranxe said.

'What is mastering magic?' Semester asked.

'When you will no more require any conventional way of doing any magic. You will be that stock of energy that can do anything just like we can think anything. You need a lot of research and hard work and evolution and mind work to achieve that state, but those will be your last researches, or hard work. Now back to work,' Master Lacranxe said, 'let me help you with the chants and the energy building. If you have it in you, nothing shall stop you.'

Right after coming out of Master Lacranxe's house, David and Semester had to, as had been directed to them, report that Zolahart was the one to have kidnapped Semester.

'Well since he knew we have the dash, he definitely understood a few contents of it a little more,' Semester said.

'Not a danger I guess,' David said, 'I respect his wisdom.'

'Well anyway, at least we know that "energy" is the core of it all, and that's where we have to hit,' Semester said, 'was that lesson really helpful?'

'It is difficult for me to figure out what purpose he called us for,' David said.

'Why?' Semester asked.

'He knows too much,' David said, 'supposedly not having read either of the Prohibited books, he knows their contents, he knows Zolahart is alive, he knows Sir Paradis is there, and he told us to reveal that Zolahart is alive, despite knowing that the Head of the Atz galaxy has forbidden us to.'

'You're right,' Semester said, 'there's much that we both don't know.'

Semester and David didn't have to wait very long and were attended shortly by an Officer of the Sovereign Authority of the Universe. Fuelling hopes, David found it was Officer Kollin.

'Zolahart is alive,' David hit the punch line. 'He had kidnapped Semester, and washed her memories.'

Officer Kollin held his head and then looked up, biting his lips as if trying hard to be patient. 'I am not interested,' he said (the hopes . . .)

'He had or has the Prohibited book,' David continued, 'possibly the one that was stolen a slout ago, and he-is-eternal.'

'Eternal? Hah . . .' Officer Kollin looked here and there expecting others in the office to start laughing so that he would then join in. 'So you firstly mean to tell me you had a dream about the contents of the Prohibited book, and secondly you want to tell me Zolahart is alive and . . . huh . . .', he sighed.

'Sir Atz told me not to reveal this truth to anyone,' David said, 'He saw the truth in his truth test.'

'Just another truth test, Master David,' Officer Kollin said, 'if you are found to correct, Sir Atz is going to be here, to justify why he asked you not to let this out, failing which, I promise you, he will be under . . . probation.' He then turned and shouted, 'you heard me buddies?'

CHAPTER 25

SHOWDOWN

Semester and David saw Justin after a long time, and almost did not recognize him.

Justin looked exhausted and mistreated.

'Well, he better be,' Semester said, still not over with the matter.

'There were earlier speculations that Sir Atz will be summoned,' a tall woman said in a constant, flat tone. 'But that might worsen the matter if Sir Atz really is close to Zolahart. During these times shielding up and getting lost is common.'

'You mean Laurins?' another counterpart, a man sitting next to her said.

Justin was seated at the back corner of the room; two ferocious personals in their now familiar black uniform were standing on both sides of him. The security parameters looked high and David and Semester wondered they had been keeping the reason of all this as a secret.

'You think we can plan against the Head of the Galaxy?' the man continued, 'without him knowing about it? It's better if he is summoned. We can already look at the ratio of those required to be present here in the meeting, and those actually present at the meeting. I can't even trust you on that matter, and nor do I tell you to trust me. This can not be a secret mission.'

'I do not know, sir and madam,' David said, getting up all of a sudden. Semester did not get up and waited to know whether David was actually planning to leave.

'I just had to reach a non-government investigation and tell.' David continued, 'but now it looks the same, a government meeting and interrogation and . . .' (Semester got up.)

'But that's how things work on a large scale and when decisions are not personal, I thought you were as mature as you should be by now,' the woman said.

'Well, I don't have a problem with that opinion,' David said. 'Can we leave?'

'For now, you may,' the man said, not arguing further.

Glad at realising that leaving was so simple; David and Semester turned and walked out, Semester being the one to leave without looking at Justin.

As they walked down the narrow corridor, Semester and David talked about unimportant things. Everyone was doing their own work.

'And my mum was like . . . mmmm', David said, pursing his lips so hard that they almost entirely vanished inside.

'Shut up,' Semester said, 'it's better to be quiet than to open your mouth speaking nonsense.' Semester said.

'Hang on, you mean she talks nonsense?'

'Oh no! I meant she . . . I meant she has wisdom,' Semester said, 'you are such a . . . . what happened?' She noticed David's attention very slowly scattered from the conversation to the things around, he looked up and then went silent, slowly observing the area from left to right like there was a river flowing to that direction and only he could see it.

'What happened?' Semester said.

'Nothing,' David said, 'it was . . . it just took a lil attention. This was a very clear example of when you feel like you are in the same space and time for the second time.'

Semester shook her head, 'wha . . .!' and sighed.

They took the Quixie flier and David resumed his talk, 'so dad collected all his documents and stuff, and smiled and . . . I felt like laughing at him. Sorry.'

'Oh god,' Semester said, 'anyway, I am tensed.'

'Straight to your room,' David said, pointing his finger as they reached Semester's house.

'Hmm.'

'Yes you should be, but nottt . . .' David's voice died out as he saw Aunt Rose staring at them right in the middle of their way.

'Hello . . .' David murmured.

'Hello.' Rose said, giving a harsh look at Semester and walking away.

David raised his eye brows and tip-toed with Semester to her room.

'I can understand,' David said, reacting to Rose's routinely check-out. 'That could have been worse for other parents. I like her.'

'Yeah she's the bestest.' Semester said, winking. 'What happened now?'

David had this time focused his eyes on a small pink something hanging at a wall.

'Nothing,' David said, walking closer to the wall.

The pink something moved a little, on its own.

'What the-' Semester said.

The pink something moved again and fell off. Then following the other sounds, David and Semester found that almost everything in the room was moving, as if the floor was quaking.

'What—!' Semester whimpered.

'Oh my!' David said.

Semester went towards the door to open it, but David held her hand and stopped her.

'What are you doing?' Semester said, not looking pleased.

Then, Sir Atz appeared right in front of them, in Semester's room.

'This is not . . . .' Semester whispered.

'This . . . !' David said, his face looking like he had an extensive urge to tell something, but the priority had to be switched as the powerful man who they had just complained about was standing right in front of them.

'This is my room . . .' Semester said.

Sir Atz smirked and clicked his fingers; the room was lost in utter darkness.

Semester and David groped for each other's hands and ensured they were together.

'What is this?' Semester almost shouted.

The lights went on once again, but the room was still lost—it was a new place.

'It's not,' Sir Atz said, '-your room.'

David and Semester, both familiar with what greenish and smoggy environment could mean, looked into each other's eyes and said, 'were we ready enough . . . ?'

'This was what I saw that blay,' David whispered, 'when we were practicing combat and I had a vision. This was just it, just the same.'

They were in some location of Zolahart, with a new editions of Joz's standing around.

'Hello everyone,' Atz said to all of them, 'I am back. Are you both done with the observation?' he said, to David and Semester, 'because I hope not, that'll mean you have a very poor observation.'

David and Semester made confused faces and then they spotted a man shielded and almost tied up to motionlessness, and it was Laurins.

'He . . .' was all that David said.

Semester was waiting for Atz to begin on his own, at the same time feeling the countdown of a do or die face off.

'Like you, this man felt that I worked for Sir Chief Zolahart; well I do!' Sir Atz said, 'he even stole the Prohibited book from my coffers, well. And another foolish harmless friend of yours, so useless that this innocent man could not even ask her to understand the situation or trust his righteousness. Here he is. Don't strain your eyes, you won't still be able to see his deformed face. He is waiting for the procedure of his legal ending . . . the ending of his pain and adventure unnecessary intelligence. Now what about you two? Semester, who never did anything apart from earning hatred from Sir Zolahart, and you, David, who DID-NOT-MEET-SIR-ZOLAHART flaunts his rescuing abilities!'

'Well in any case it was ultimately me at the hands of whom this had to take place,' David said, not letting his surprise at the fact that Atz, and so probably Zolahart knew he had not met Zolahart in the process of rescuing Semester.

Meanwhile, Semester kept silent, and alarmed.

'Were you really not bothered of me, why would you have me fired . . . ?' David taunted.

'Aah, not only fired,' Sir Atz said, 'I also did not let you be appointed as a very senior official, which you genuinely deserved.'

'Oh my . . .' David said in a sarcastic tone, 'am I really that hazardous?'

'Well, I don't have to think you can bother me until I can control things in your life like puppets, no?'

'How correct—"until" you can,' David said.

Sir Atz smirked again.

'We want to leave or enter?' Semester said, one last time finalising their stance.

'Enter,' David said, 'that's only what we will look forward to.'

Semester nodded.

'So where is your . . . Sir Zolahart and the Prohibited book that he owes his life to?'

'You better mind that tongue that you want to keep safe,' Sir Atz said. 'You have no idea of certain things.'

'Yeah . . . so what next?' Semester asked.

'Let me complete!' Atz said in a funny requesting tone, 'though I am an important being over here, master Zolahart never told me who there was in your disguise, David. To escape him and take Joz along?'

'He didn't tell you because he himself would be unaware,' David said.

'I wonder, but you see someone very rare told him the name,' Atz said.

'Are you here to boast about facts that do not surprise us?' Semester said, 'because those who have such facts do not boast, take us, for example.'

'No no no,' Atz said, don't be in a hurry when you are here this time.

'Can we save him?' Semester whispered to David, pointing at Laurins, who could barely lift his head up.

'Yes,' David said.

'Take me back to the Office,' Semester said, but no Quixie flier worked. 'Okay,' Semester said, 'try destroying the shields?'

David said, 'take care that I am not attacked,' and closed his eyes.

Semester qiuckly stepped forward and looked into Atz's eyes, hypnotizing him. Atz immediately came altogether to a halt and even his eyes did not blink anymore.

'Hey girl!' A dark haired woman looking absolutely wicked jumped forward and Semester decided not to hypnotise her, guessing that she could hypnotise around four at maximum.

But sadly, two men and two women swooshed towards her like they had propellers fitted to their butt and held her, also blocking her view.

Semester realised no one present there lacked unconventional skills.

Semester personally struggled to put them aside. She tried to turn and see if David was safe and undisturbed, but could not. Someone hit with a hand blow near her neck and it was painful. She somehow freed one of her wrists and held her band that was on the other wrist. One of the two women was thrown to some distance, but for no good. It did not even look like a fight. The situation looked well under-control of the opposition to Semester. She tried to blind them by trying to throw hot and intense white light, but as she was about to do so, she felt the grips on her arms getting loose.

There were not one, or two, or three, or even four, but a total of five Davids that she could see, one tackling a man, and four others looking on, and being looked on.

Semester shut her eyes, and muttered spells; she floated up and gathered her core energy, all the Davids still looked on and the real one could not be distinguished.

All the shields broke down and Semester's band almost constricted her hand as a result of exertion due to its energy.

'The government is not so lame,' came a new voice.

Very surprisingly, it was Officer Korr, with his investigation officers, and even governmental aids with him.

Though not in the condition of making any more sarcastic comments, Atz said, 'in that case I wonder what took you so long. Waiting for the girl to do it for you?'

'I am sorry, but not here to talk,' Officer Kollin said, and there began the fierce combat. All the Kollin army took on Atz army, Kollin probably took on Atz, Semester and all the Davids took to anyone available.

'No!' Semester's shriek pierced everyone's ear drums as she saw one of the David crushed by Atz.

'That could be me . . .' the real David muttered as he conveyed to Semester with his expressions that he was still fine. 'Let me see how they do it,' he said, as he on-the-spot experimented doing the same.

Atz held his band and the ceiling began to fall.

'What the hell is he doing!?' Semester said, 'even his own team will be hurt . . .'

'One—Atz did not do it, Laurins just ended, two, I guess not that our enemies will be hurt!' David shouted as he held Semester's hand and made her notice that there was no single enemy left around under the falling hall.

'Take us out of here!' he shouted.

"Out of here" meant just outside the falling Location. The situation was so pathetic that even the Infolet Department had started arriving.

'Where did he go!?' Semester said.

David hunted for a reply as he saw the rescue team taking out those under the debris. Thinking that Atz might not have yet shielded himself up again, Semester tried reaching him and it worked, soon after they reached a place, but there was no one and nothing around. Then all of a sudden a green shield surrounded them and about a hundred men and women appeared around them.

Two Davids that he had left behind too arrived and they saw no point in standing still and get shielded even before they got a chance to do something, so they began attacking.

'You know,' the real David said to Semester, 'I think there is a Location here. Just right here. And Atz is in there. We can't see it. Can you break green shields too?'

'I think we can,' Semester said.

CHAPTER 26

FINISHED

A serious situation.

David and Semester stood alone, surrounded by a swarm of deadly rivals. Yes, two more Davids keeping around four or six of them engaged.

'The game is not so simple,' David said, 'what just happened was because they did not have an idea of what we knew, but what lies next is the real thing.'

'Whatever be it, this is where we have to begin,' Semester said.

David and Semester held their respective bands at once and spelled the hymns together, but could cause no harm to the shield.

'The attacks not always add up,' David inferred.

'Are we missing right now? From others' point of view?' Semester asked him.

'No, that's when someone else shields you over your self constructed shield,' David replied, 'proving that you volunteered to enter the Bacon.'

While David was saying this, the enemies present outside hit him altogether and the impact was severe. For long, David could not even open his eyes, then he said, 'I was just coming to the point that we're talking too much!'

Semester threw light all around and everything outside the shield got hidden. She then held her right arm up and though not audible, she strained her throat commendably as she angrily repeated the mantras. The shield broke off and David joined her in shielding most of the enemies.

'The new report is—your anger can work for good, eh?' David said.

Much to his relief, David's two alter egos were doing commendably well.

'Hey there,' David shouted at one of them, 'find out if we are near a location, 'cause I really suppose so.' Then, David shielded himself and focused.

'David!' Semester's scream was heard. Four men had bound Semester in chains and were about to carry her away.

The other alter ego of David shut his eyes too and cast virtual Bacons towards the men. The pink colored virtual Bacons that emanated from his band ran towards their target and faster than the men could escape, they tore their limbs apart, spattering much blue blood around.

Semester regained her self control and vigor quickly and hypnotized a man who she saw was targeting the real David who was still focusing. Before she could do anything, the man attacked David's shield and the shield broke off at once.

'What the—they can break'em, so easily!' Semester muttered and then distracted the man by throwing an iron head onto his head. As soon as the man looked at her, she hypnotized him and made him twist his own arm beyond permissible limits. Then, she felt she could do better with it.

She ordered the man, through her eyes, to run up to her. The man quickly obeyed.

Unable to remove her eye contact and see whether David was safe, she shouted, 'David! I am not watching you! Open your eyes!'

Very sure that David was unable to listen to her through his supernatural focus, she said to the other Davids, any one of which would hopefully hear, 'disturb his focus! Now!'

By the time she had said this, the man had obeyed Semester's instruction and he stopped in front of her.

'Is there a location around here?' she asked.

'Yes,' the man said.

'Is that where Atz is?' she asked again, in an extreme hurry to know all she could before she missed the opportune moment.

'I don't know,' the man answered.

'What's in there?' Semester asked.

'The Prohibited book,' the man answered.

'What!?' Semester exclaimed to herself.

'The Prohibited book,' the hallucinated man repeated.

'What else do you know about it? Wha-what is-what's it?' Semester stammered.

'It is the residence to Sir Chief Zolahart, the eternal Mater of the Universe.'

Semster's mouth fell open and remained in that awe-stuck condition, then she held her band and threw that man away and looked at David, but there were only two Davids now, either one of two duplicates was absent, or the original was.

One of them was floating little higher than everyone else and the other seemed to be in danger, and surrounded by around eleven enemies he was showering virtual meteorites to scare off the enemy.

Semester floated high and a meteorite narrowly missed her.

The third David suddenly appeared on her way and said, 'I tried to imitate Zolahart's personality but failed.'

'Shut up!' Semester shouted, 'I hypnotized one of these and he told me we are next to Zolahart's residence, and the Prohibited book is there too.'

'All you knew was hypnotizing but I never knew it could actually be put to use,' David said.

'Very foolish on Atz part to fly here,' Semester said but both of them were shielded again by all the enemy army below them.

'No . . .' Semester said, as she saw as many shields forming around them as there were number of enemies.

'Now will you be taken inside,' shouted a woman coming closer.

The Location one became visible slowly. What was beyond belief now became clear.

A huge green structure, named immediately by David "The Dark Senate", stood at a little distance. Its smog was calm and slow and the area looked still, looking quite funnily contrary to the disordered battlefield.

To the shielded David and Semester who floated above looked down again. From their aerial view, the other two Davids, looked like they were hopping unnecessarily.

On noticing carefully, it appeared that the smog was shaping itself into something that roughly looked like two smoggy limbs creeping from behind the Location.

'First of all this little chirpet's eyes should be taken care off, they do a lot of talking,' a woman said, 'you are not the only one with indigenous magic.' She shut her eyes to avoid eye contact with Semester and breathed deep, then she blew towards Semester and David. Semester held her band and muttered spells quickly and destroyed one shield. But there were around fifty more.

'Let us do that again' the woman said, on failing at her first trial.

'That is . . . !' David said, pointing to the entrance of the Location. Everyone turned.

It was Zolahart. He appeared at the gate, very calmly, looking unmoved and easy towards the situation, and turned and went inside. All that could be seen was a flowing dark shroud and his odd complexion.

'He just went inside!' the David with Semester said to her.

'Do something!' Semester said.

'This virtual band won't be as powerful in breaking these stong green shields,' David said?

'Virtual band? Are you one of the unreal Davids?' Semester said.

'Yes! The real David is there . . .' David said, pointing below right, where two Davids still looked like they were hopping. Well, actually just one. One of the Davids, the real one, was lying on his knees, focusing.

'Watch out!' a man said, pointing at him and then he punched David at the back.

'Watch out!' other men and women shouted and attacked David physically. The other David alone tried his best to tackle them, but . . . looked like hopping.

Soon, a small yellow cyclone was conjured up, David was deep in focus, much to being numb to physical pains and the cyclone grew intense. David opened his eyes and stood up. While everything and everyone around was swayed here and there by the cyclone, David stood firm and strong looking like an unbeatable hero of the unjust climax in a movie. But the real situation was not so inequitable; David kept his focus and eyes concentrated at the location, where things still appeared calm. The smoggy limbs, though, retreated slowly as if the non-living had consciousness about what was going on.

'What are you doing?' the unreal David next to her asked Semester.

'Sending him my vibes,' Semester said, looking at David and teleporting her energy 'what he's doing might need so much of energy!'

The replica David looked at Semester and then his real heroic self and said, 'stop it! I am not requiring it. You think I am making a cyclone? That's all?'

Semester held her breath and looked at David with eyes full of trust. A lot of noise continued to come from the muddled cyclonic site. David remained still, his shirt clinging to his chest and his good hair being brushed by the winds of the storm.

Semester anyhow singled out the time to mutter, 'he does look smart.'

The David standing next to her replied, 'you can have a closer look over here.'

'Shut . . .'

The big bang noise that followed proved all the preceding noise to be hollow. David had wretched the whole of Location one that now gusted with a dynamic explosion. Nothing that fell out really fell anywhere as it got destroyed completely.

By this time the place where the location stood was completely vacant. No debris, nothing. All matter converted into energy; let us not bring Einstein in here though.

David's stupendous performance filled Semester with ebullience and passion. She shut her eyes and muttered "éspéeada ereahva". A glistening sword appeared in her hands and she hit the inner few shields that began breaking off like they were made of glass.

The momentary deafening noise had demarked the much needed destruction on the word of the prohibited guidelines. Finished.

CHAPTER 27

"LOOKS LIKE" PEACE

The sacrifice of Sir Laurins was being commemorated first and foremost in the Outer Senate of the Atz.

David, Semester, Rose, Peter ...well it is better to say that Miss Viniah was present, implying that all others were too.

'Some Subroto wanting to meet you,' Romella said to David.

'I see,' David said, 'will just be back,' and he made his way through the elite crowd.

'I am Subroto,' Subroto said as David looked out for him.

'Hello Subroto,' David greeted.

'Master of the Universe, Sir Omen has sent this message to you,' Subroto said, 'it's handwritten,' he clapped with joy.

'Wow, Subroto,' David said, smiling at his reaction. 'Thank you.'

'Thank you.' Subroto said.

'Oh, of course, convey my high high regards and gratitude to him. I am really feeling privileged.'

'Sure,' Subroto said, leaving.

'Ouch,' David said, as Semester pinched him.

'Tending to be a gentleman haa?' she said, 'what's that?' she asked looking at the small frame.

'What's-that!?' David said.

'What?'

'What are you wearing?' David said, 'it looks so girly and ...and formal.'

'Shut up,' Semester said. 'I can do what I want, dare you interfere in such matters.'

'Oh well, that's a message from Sir Omen' David said, coming back to the point.

'Oh my!' Semester said, 'isn't it at all for me?'

'Well I think your name is mentioned here,' David said, 'but since I am the third Official in Atz in seniority, it is addressed and sent for me.'

'Ooooh. Okay...' Semester said, starting to read it with David.

Officer David 15,

Type two Office

Atz

I congratulate you hereby and am delighted zat you performed your zpiritual dutiez to ze bezt of your abilitiez, wiz good accountability and nerve. Ze lozz of a leader, Zir Laurinz iz irreparable and an unavoidable fault; candidly. But we ought to acknowledge Mazter Lacranxe, and my own advizor Mazter Hebrew to keep my attention never deviate from ze doubtful matter. Ze deal unveiled hereby iz zat even if ze two zoulz were true to you, but zey wouldn't unwizely chooze to die by attempting to steal a Prohibited book in return of being zave from dying. Zey genuinely owe it to you zat you zave zeir livez, but it iz time for "zoul mitigation" az Mazter Lacranxe told me. He alzo told me jokingly to tell you zat you ought not to not worry, az neizer 'I' nor Mazter Hebrew knowz what exactly happened. Writing ziz letter waz a tough job az I had to memorize certain termz and eventz zat I did not underztand.

Anyhow, "zoul mitigation" haz to happen at your handz, and I zink I am told to tell you to "feel free." Before I get any more confuzed, I would not forget to congratulate Mizz Zemezter 15 for being extraordinary all over. I would be glad if zhe beautifiez ze government by becoming a part of it.

Yourz,

Omen

'Oh look,' David said, 'invited for being an Official, directy by the Master! Not bad, Sim.'

'Oh no, officials are boring people.' Semester replied, checking out David, 'Oh, er...bt yeah, that's cool.'

'Time to give the book back I guess,' David said.

'Soul mitigation!' Semester said, 'sounds a real task.'

'Are you okay with me, aunt rose?' David stepped aside and said to Semester's mom.

'Er, I think all I cared for was your safety, and your unnecessary poking around. But, I guess it was necessary. God bless.' Rose said, smiling.

'Where are you going?' Semester asked David. 'You are supposed to be present here.'

'Oh yeah, she's right.' Officer Kollin said.

'Officer!' David greeted, 'nice to meet you. And thanks a lot. A lot.'

'Well I did my job while you did my job.' Kollin said.

'Oh no, we were just trying to save our lives.' David replied.

'What exactly was it though?' Kollin asked.

'Well,' David said, 'Atz and Zolahart and their stolen Book were inside. And they all were just destroyed.'

'Whoa,' Kollin said, 'what guarantees that they were inside and had not fleed.'

'Well, I can not guarantee the book,' David said, 'but yes, since it is an irreversible process, the destroyer has to be sure that the target includes what is required, and does not include what is not required- just the right casualties So I could sense, the magic helped me sense, in fact almost see through the walls, the living spirits present in my target area. And there they were. I guarantee that.'

'That's super cool, why don't you teach me?' Kollin said.

'Well, I think I should leave,' David said, smiling.

'Am I supposed to come?' Semester asked.

'Of course, silly. I can't fell so free just because I am told to,' David said, 'you will have to read.'

'I can't read it!' Semester said, looking deep into the Prohibited book under the section "soul mitigation". 'Some very weird symbols. They're not even words.'

'Really?' David said, facing the other side and his eyes shut. 'Er, there must be something?'

'Hang on yes, I can see' Semester said, 'It says, at the end, that these are not words, these are conscious symbols. They create a conscious picture and souls can read them alone.'

'But you do have certain powers as far as consciousness is concerned. You should have been able to read it.'

'No,' Semester said.

'I got it,' David said.

'What?'

'We have to handle the book back to the souls.'

'Oh my god!' Semester said, 'does that mean they will become like us?'

'I strictly don't think so,' David said.

'Better than us?' Semester said, making a sound that impelled David to feel she could get tearful.

'Just pack it up,' David said. 'I'm going.'

'Where?'

'Can you hear that?' David said.

'What? Oh, the knock, someone's at the door.' Semester said, 'coming.'

David sat back and said to himself, 'can the Quixie flier take me to the place, if I simply tell it to take me where Paradis had captured Joz, near the ancient ruins...I think that's where he gave the souls the... ice.'

'You don't have to go anywhere,' Semester said, coming in again, 'they're here. In my house!'

From behind her, entered the small boyfriend and girlfriend souls, ready to take the Book back.

'So that was an untold deal,' David said, 'not fair.'

'But there was a purpose we did not tell you about it,' the boy said.

'And it is?'

'None of us could be sure that the book could be wisely used and safely returned, it should not have looked like we are mortgaging it. '

'Don't try to fool me again', David said, 'whether it looks like or not, doesn't matter, you did mortgage it. Tell me the reason.'

'Well, you knew the deal, didn't you?' the soul said, looking afraid of having said so.

'Er...what?' David said.

'Er....yes?' Semester said, resting her hand on her waist and looking suspiciously at David.

'Well I'm not Justin,' David said, 'don't give me that look.'

'Shut up. Tell me now!' Semester said.

'Well, I had another vision. Of this same boy meeting Sir Lacranxe and talking about some deal...'

'Wow,' Semester said, 'and you didn't tell me.'

'Why would I?' David pacified, 'until I saw one of the two visions come true, I didn't have any idea that they were reality.'

'Er...so you'll take the book all by yourself?' Semester asked the souls.

'Yes,' the girl said, 'just as we had brought it, all by ours...' she stopped, in a reflex shutting her mouth with her own hands.

Semester stared at the girl and then picked up the heavy book, and handed it over.

'Hey, how is it going to benefit you?' David asked.

'We will no more need ice,' the boy said, in tears. His girlfriend too, looking even more emotional.

'Oh okay okay...' David said, 'thank you.'

With synchronous pops, the souls disappeared.

'I won't say that was not great,' Semester said, 'but yet an okayish reward, no?'

'The..re..' Semester said, as her room began getting dimly yellowish; and then a transparent image of Sir Paradis appeared in front of them.

'Oh my God!' Semester said, 'I...'

David remained silent, his head held straight, he looked up to Paradis.

'Good time precious ones,' Paradis said. His warm beautiful voice soothed the aura. 'The visions, David. You know not what a cycle of the Universe means. But being born exactly one cycle after me, is equivalent to being my direct descendent. Though not voluntarily possible, you will have visions that will turn into reality. Without or in your presence.'

'What about me?' Semester said. 'Who am I?'

'Semester, a precious child of the Universe, do the needed, worry not about the results.'

'Sir, I could see Atz and Zolahart. I...'

'Respect the enemy that you ever fear,' Paradis said. 'Until you are great enough not to sound intentionally disrespectful.'

'Eh?' David mumbled. 'Sorry. Sir Atz and Sir Zolahart were in there. I could almost see them. So, is it ...I mean, Sir Zolahart has really ended?'

The biggest fear of David's then turned into reality.

Sir Paradis vanished and David's question was left unanswered. Well much to everyone's fear, Paradis had answered the question on his very first meeting with David and Semester.

Great philosophies and truths must always be remembered

End and eternity remain the final things...

PART 2

✦
✦ ✦

MAN IN THE UNIVERSE—A 21ST CENTURY APPRAISAL

Francis A. Andrew.

I would like to point out that the use of the word "man" in the title of Sir Fred Hoyle's work, was a common form of parlance for "humankind" in the 1960's when the book was written, and so does not connotate anything of a sexist nature.

"In the beginning God created heaven, and earth." This, the first verse from the first chapter of the first book in the Bible clearly indicates that God brought into being two dimensions of creation— one spiritual and one material. It is the spiritual one which Aishwarya Pandey so aptly captures in her story Cosmic Colossal. In an attempt to both contrast and compare the spiritual and material universes, I have chosen to write an appraisal of Sir Fred Hoyle's 1966 book, "Man in the Universe," and to investigate how much of Hoyle's analyses of the various issues facing mankind in the timeframe in which he composed this work can still be found to be relevant in the first quarter of the 21st century. The book, "Man in the Universe," is based upon the Bampton Lectures in America Series, delivered by Professor Hoyle at Columbia University in 1966.

In the first lecture in the series, Hoyle looked at the association of the space programme with astronomical research and very interestingly related this issue to the attitudes towards education during the years of the Great Depression and the relative affluence of the post-war years. As a general backdrop to his analysis, Hoyle described the fundamental tenets of the Keynesian economic model with its emphasis on economic stimulation regardless of the intrinsic value of the projects undertaken to effect this stimulation—digging ". . . . large holes in the ground, and . . . . filling them in again" (p. 3). As prosperity seemed to be an unattainable dream during the Depression era, the focus of students would be concentrated upon their areas of interest. Contrariwise, students in the post-war era regard their time at university in the purely utilitarian consideration of it being a "meal ticket" (P.2).This prevailing attitude has had the knock-on effect of justifying the space programme in terms of its usefulness, and that its acceptability among the general public stems from its ". . . . being presented as a species of astronomical crusade" (p.2).

Hoyle's examination of the economic factors concerning the space programme does not seem to offer any justification for the resources allocated to this programme. If national productivity were given a factor of 1,000 units, then resource allocation for large scale projects, such as space research, should only be between 1 and 10 for the larger and wealthier nations but no more than 1 for the smaller and less developed nations. Misallocations over the aforementioned maximum units may be productive of distortions due to the large project turning out results below expectation and the non-maximisation of the smaller projects due to lack of sufficient funding.

Hoyle returns to the issue of the linkage of the connection between the space programme and astronomical research by giving due consideration to the factors that impede ground based observation and limit the advantages of observational equipment in high Earth orbit. Yet, after having given due consideration to the problems which beset terrestrial astronomy—such as light pollution, industrial pollution, full moons, cloud and meteorological conditions—he notes that 95% of astronomical information is derived from ground based equipment.

Of course, this was in 1966; since then we have had the Hubble and Kepler telescopes in operation sending back vast amounts of information and greatly expanding our knowledge of the Universe. So, the question may now be—does this 95% figure still stand in 2013 (at the time of writing)? Although Hubble and Kepler have been highly productive, about 60 new ground-based telescopes have been built since Hoyle first delivered his lecture back in 1966. So there are now 60 large ground based instruments in 2013 as opposed to only around six in 1966. While no figures are readily available, it would seem that this percentage figure still holds—more or less.

While touching upon the utility value of astronomy and its relationship to the space programme, Hoyle points out that the space programme consumes around 1% of the US's GNP. Yet for only one fifth of the cost of the space programme in one year, 100 new 200 inch reflecting telescopes could be built on the ground. But if present day society has no interest in astronomy, then, says Hoyle, it should be dropped from all talk concerning the space programme.

The spill-over from the "utilitarianisation" of education is not only into the space programme, but can be seen to have affected the issue of grant allocations for scientific projects. Hoyle points out that in the competition between the abstract and the material for scarce resources, funding priorities will always favour the material: this basically means constructing greater numbers of machines. "It is more or less irrelevant what the machines are used for" (p. 11). Here we can notice a linear movement from Keynesian economics, to education, to research funding, which eventually plays itself out in a vicious circle which returns to the Keynesian mode of economic operation referred to above. Hoyle avers that this priority ought to be reversed in favour of the abstract, as machines are the products of the abstract ideas we have in mind: "destroy every machine on Earth, and within quite a short time our modern civilization would be reconstructed, due to the ideas we have in our heads" (p. 11).

It is interesting to note that in spite of such events as "the collapse of communism," "the triumph of capitalism," "the era of Thatcherism" and so forth, the utilitarianism which continues to pervade education and its over-spill into research funding, the ghost of John Maynard Keynes still stalks the halls of national treasuries and economic planning fora!

Yet, it is not too difficult to discern a contradiction in the modern utilitarian manner of thinking. The public will query the "usefulness" of the space programme and astronomy, but not the "digging of holes and the filling of them in" as a means of achieving "economic stimulation." If, to a fairly reasonable degree, awareness of this contradiction pervaded the public consciousness, then corrective measures in restoring a balance between the material and the abstract could be beneficial for the advancement of science.

Although an astronomer, Hoyle explained that scientists of all disciplines must accept the prime importance of physics. An example he gave to demonstrate this point was in an imaginary case whereby he were forced to choose between funding for a telescope and funding for a particle accelerator (p. 13). His choice of the latter rested on the premise that discoveries in the laws of physics preceded their practical application. However, astronomy would come hot on the heels of physics, for the Universe provides for mankind a laboratory, larger than anything which can be reproduced terrestrially, whereby these laws can be demonstrated. If those who wonder as to why God created such a vast Universe rather than merely a scaled down version involving life bearing regions, then their coming to a realisation of the utility value of a universal "laboratory" whereby the laws of physics may be studied prior to any practical application of them, will enable them to value better the importance of the abstract and its relationship with the material—but in a truly post-Keynesian context.

In Chapter 14 of Cosmic Colossal, Aishwarya Pandey describes David's experiences in a library. In his "Morcian" body, David has temporarily shed his spirit body and taken on a human one. What dovetails so well with the pre-war attitude of students referred to by Hoyle in his lecture, is David's fascination with the contents of a library which he is experiencing for the first time, as it is indicative of one forming an interest in a subject for no other reason than for the sake of interest in it. During the conversation between David and the librarian, there was no talk about education being related to such issues as jobs, future career prospects, financial gain or any other material consideration; it was a quest for knowledge as an end in itself. Perhaps, in terms of education, the two forms of attitude to learning have some form of connection to the "material" and the "abstract" Hoyle referred to, and so to the opening verse of the Book of Genesis in which ". . . . God created heaven and earth." It is these parallel aspects of creation which Ms. Pandey captures so well in her novel.

✦
✦ ✦

The second part of Sir Fred Hoyle's lecture series is entitled "Know Then Thyself." Hoyle points out that this was a precept of the ancient Greeks and a feature in a poem by Alexander Pope (English poet—1688-1744) called "Know Thyself." After some consideration being given to what one may mean by the term "God," and that He may not be subject to any kind of analytical scan, Hoyle then queries as to whether or not this may apply to man.

Hoyle states that one of the greatest discoveries of the nineteenth century was that which was made by Darwin and Wallace and which holds that man is an animal. What is most interesting in Hoyle's presentation of this discovery is that this fact had been so patently obvious all along. So why did it take so long for mankind to realise the obvious? Hoyle claims that it was the Bible which provided the "strong incentive" for people to ignore the obvious (ps. 18 & 19) but, when confronted with the obvious, people readily accepted it.

We may wish to pause at this juncture and consider Hoyle's thesis in the light of Aishwarya Pandey's novel and the concept of parallel universes mentioned above. Perhaps we could ask as to what way man is an animal. It surely has never been far from the obvious that man bears various animal functions in the realms of biology, chemistry and physiology. However, what has always been within the parameters of the obvious, and to such an extent that it has never eluded man or been denied by him, is that the human species soars in intellectual ability above its fellow creatures. This intellectual ability achieves such heights that it can grasp within the constructs of religious systems a universe beyond the material and into one which embraces the concept of the spiritual and even the notion of a supreme creator being. It is essentially this which distinguishes man from other created beings on this Earth.

Basically, Hoyle is asserting that it is cultural phenomena that block us from seeing the obvious. He further asserts that this blockage did not end in the 19th century. However, he asserts that while it is not too difficult to embrace a willingness to proceed along new lines of thought, it requires quite something more to obtain "the right lines of thought" (p. 20). An "unusual line of attack," let alone the "right line of attack," (p. 20) will not automatically present itself to one who is simply willing and able to think without prejudice. In fact, even "knowing the right line of attack," will not be of great assistance, as this knowledge must needs be put into an entirely new conceptual construction. Hoyle believes that the process which moves from a willingness to 'think outside the box' (as we say in more modern parlance), to finding the correct method of approach, to forming the correct conceptual framework in which to place it, emanates from mere chance. He avers that the opportunities to think outside of the usual patterns, occurs when, for whatever reason, these patterns dissolve and reform. It is precisely at the point of re-formation that the flashes of insight occur. It may be early in the morning upon wakening, on holiday, or in the chance remarks of someone which throws the brain into momentary confusion. However, these insightful moments are brief and fleeting (p. 21). And even if one manages to see the value of the new insight, there is still the job of convincing others of its worth (p. 24). One may well consider the role of science fiction (or any genre of fiction for that matter) in the process of the formation of original thought patterns. Does not science fiction ensure that the human mind is not held prisoner within dogmatic confines—be they of science or religion? Is the science fiction writer not attempting to take these brief insightful moments and expand them into a wider and more permanent framework called the "science fiction novel"? Does not the science fiction novel serve to restrain the rational scientific mind and cognitive processes of the scientist from becoming over-rational to such an extent that the mind is paralysed from thinking outside the box? I would answer these questions in the affirmative. Ms Pandey's novel is clearly indicative of a writer who is willing to think outside the usual boxed-in patterns; her composition raises the mind to such a level that it encompasses a parallel universe of spirit beings and so challenges the reader to at least consider that such a parallelism does in fact exist in the created order of things.

Hoyle explains that for any original thought to be worthwhile, a basic knowledge of the subject matter must be possessed by the individual experiencing the insight. Without this basic knowledge, the insight will turn out to be nonsense. Yet, he goes on to explain that in many cases, the more detailed and in-depth the technical knowledge of a subject a scientist may possess, the more readily that new idea will be killed off due to an ability on the part of the scientist to see all the possible technical snags in the practical implementation of that new idea. A new and original thought has to be carefully nurtured and treated in such a way that the "critical faculties do not bear too soon on the new idea" (p. 23). Hoyle compares new ideas to the DNA mutations in biology in the sense that most mutational DNA is junk; likewise, most new ideas are to be placed within the latter category. However, the subtle art seems to be in sorting out the good from the bad. Just as most mutations are harmful, most new ideas are too. The science fiction novel encompasses both the "junk DNA" and the "good DNA;" it is up to the scientist to tease out the good and weave it into a credible scientific fact. It is in this respect that Hoyle offers a definition of the "crank" (p. 23). A new idea must be given the chance to take root and should only be rejected after being exposed to later criticism which shows its lack of viability. The crank holds on to all ideas in spite of their having been shown to be devoid of credibility.

We could perhaps at this point distinguish between the "crank" on the one hand, and the "genius" on the other. In so doing, let us enumerate the conditions Hoyle gives for the successful acceptance of fresh and new insights:

1.) Ability to think outside cultural restraints and blocks.
2.) Getting the right line of attack on new thought processes.
3.) Recognition of the opportunity to think outside the usual thought patterns.
4.) The possession of a basic knowledge necessary for insight validity.
5.) Not to kill off the insights by an overbearance on them with the technical snags which may hamper them.
6.) To reject unfeasible ideas once they have been subject to later and reasonable amounts of critical analyses.
7.) Nurturing good ideas that are feasible.
8.) Placing the new good new idea within a conceptual framework.
9.) Convincing others of the feasibility of the new ideas.

Presented in this empirical form, it can be seen why true genius is so rare; there are so many conditions to be met in order to establish an idea emanating from the mind of a genius.

Hoyle's own "flashes of insight" (ps. 24-26), concern the biological evolution of the Earth. Life at its outset was mainly chemical. When life started moving around, chemical evolution gave way to electronic evolution. In considering Aishwarya Pandey's novel, could not electronic evolution give way to spirit evolution? According to Hoyle, one of the distinguishing features man possesses is his ability to communicate the thought processes of his brain—this is mainly achieved by sound, i.e. by spoken language (ps. 28-29). Input data can be communicated from brain to brain by means of speech. In this way Hoyle compares the human being to that of a computer. Yet Hoyle sees the spoken word as being an inadequate means of communication; "a much more direct electronic output and input from one brain to another would be preferable, ..." (p.30) but to date this method of communication still has to be achieved.

Ms. Pandey, however, touches upon spirit communication in her novel. Semester, a spirit, when given a "Mocian" body (i.e. human body), cannot hear the other spirits as they communicate through higher frequency waves. It could only be by shedding her Mocian body that Semester could hear her fellow spirits again. We see, perhaps, in this description of spirit communication, a higher and more accurate form of input and output transference by sentient beings. No doubt, through science fiction, Ms. Pandey is touching upon a future form of data transference which improves upon the crudities and inaccuracies of the spoken word as described by Hoyle.

Hoyle points out that some physicists claim that subjective experience is illusory and that there is no such a thing as the present (p. 32). Yet, as he further points out, these same physicists have no compunction in applying their own subjective interpretation to the results of experiments. Nevertheless, Hoyle envisages the very role of consciousness as being to interpret the subjective present. An abandonment of this role would be tantamount to an abandonment of physics (ps 32-33). In fact, he goes on to demonstrate that human organisation and societal functionality would be possible without this form of analysing the subjective present. The events that form the subjective present in a person's life are taken from a sub-class of the totality of an individual life (p. 33). Yet in terms of trying to define this sub-class, Hoyle confesses that he can offer no solution—only the suggestion that a "series of markers" similar to full-stops which divide the sentences in written texts are needed. These "markers" have the function of dividing cause and effect for where these two phenomena are continuous "there is no possibility of dividing up the full totality of our experience" (p.34).

In attempting a solution to this problem, Hoyle examines the quantum effect whereby a physical system within the same conditions may do different things at different times—this is the Uncertainty Principle. While at one time it was believed by physicists that this uncertainty occurred by the very fact of the observer's interference (simply by means of observing), this notion had been abandoned by modern day physicists in favour of the idea that the uncertainty arose from the inaccuracies and fallibilities of human calculation (ps 34 & 35).

Hoyle finishes up on this lecture by considering time symmetry in the laws of physics (ps. 35-37). He explains how a series of events can proceed from a line going from future to past just as it is possible to move in the more usual way from past to future. The example he furnishes to demonstrate this point is a kettle of cold water being placed on a cooker. The initial state of cold water proceeds to hot water, but there is no reason why the reverse should not be the case. The challenge for thermodynamicists is to explain why only this one initial state is possible in the real world. Hoyle avers that it is "external conditions" (p. 36) that hold the key. ". . . . this becomes a cosmological problem involving the whole Universe" (p. 36). Hoyle then explains the sense of time and the subjective present as phenomena which are built into the wider cosmological context. He goes on to suggest that the uncertainty arises out of a failure of human calculations, and that this failure is due to our isolation of physical systems from the rest of the Universe. This principle, by extension, applies to ourselves; we cannot attempt to successfully explain the human phenomenon in a state of its detachment from the Universe (ps 36-37).

By writing a science fiction whose main characters are spirit entities, Aishwarya Pandey perhaps captures an essential essence in man, one which is overlooked by mainstream scientists. This is the spirit, and indeed, spiritual essence of man. That the two may overlap can be seen by David's experiences on Earth while in his Mocian body. Is this overlap somehow synonymous with that of physics and metaphysics? If so, then to divorce from the attempts to find a solution to the problem of uncertainty, the overlap between the material and the spiritual in man, can only be seen as a major procedural flaw.

✦
✦ ✦

In the third part of his lecture series, Hoyle goes on to consider whether or not it is possible to be rid of the subjective present, providing ": . . . . we suppose the existence of a *choice machine*" (p.38). While consciousness proceeds in a "smooth flow" from past to present to future, there is every reason to argue that it is composed of discreet units of cause and effect which may be selected in any order by this hypothetical choice machine and presented as time proceeding in "an ever flowing stream" (p. 39). Hoyle believes that the substitution of a choice machine for the subjective present is essential ". . . . if the quantum theory is to have logical consistency" (p. 39).

Hoyle dismisses the classical macroscopic system in quantum theory and argues that such systems are not classical at all but rather ". . . . quantum systems containing more particles than a microscopic system . . . ." (p. 40). Using the hypothetical experiment of Schrodinger's cat, Hoyle explains that a "classical apparatus" with a human observer is set up so that an event will occur if certain nuclei undergo radioactive decay and that another event will occur if there is no decay (p. 42). Although at this stage, no human involvement takes place, it is only by "taking a look" that we "condense the wave function." Without this observation, there will be "a loss of information." Only by observation can we determine if a trail of decay is there, and only by "lifting the lid" can we determine if Schrodinger's cat is alive or dead (p.42). It is through this exercise of our consciousness that human beings *can act as choice machines*" (p.42).

✦
✦ ✦

In the penultimate lecture in his series, Hoyle takes another, but more in-depth look at the issue of education, and goes on to compare and counterpoint it with research. The first anomaly that Hoyle brings to our attention is the fact that between the ages of five and twenty, very little is required or expected of the child in terms of hard and diligent work. However, from the age of about 20, the standards expected from a student at university exceed everything that was expected from him at the lower levels of education. This mal-distribution of effort is something which Hoyle believed had to be addressed.

Hoyle states that anyone reminiscing on a "misspent life" (p.48) will think on missed opportunities in education rather than in any disadvantages of birth. The reason for this is essentially that education has now become a boom industry. Jobs that could have been performed quite satisfactorily without any education, now require college degrees. "Noteworthy as this may seem, it may still only be quite small compared to what is to come in the future" (p.49). In this, Hoyle's prediction was correct; most employers in the first half of the 21st century are demanding college education from would-be employees as a prerequisite for recruitment. He was also correct in predicting the burgeoning of educational institutions and courses. Today one can acquire degrees in almost anything. Furthermore, skills such as Nursing and Hotel Management, which were once acquired *in situ* are now part of the standard university curriculum. Yet surely the best place to acquire hotel managements skills is in a hotel, and the best place for the training of nurses is in a hospital. Yet, the hotel manager and the nurse who did their training at university will be considered as being superior in their abilities than their colleagues who trained respectively in hotels and hospitals!

The main function in the expansion of education is an economic one. It is a kind of Keynesian "digging holes and filling them in again" (p.50) as a governmental means of avoiding the extremes of boom and slump. Hoyle avers that defence spending has now reached such a saturation point—in that the world can kill itself so many times over—that spending in this area as a means of achieving economic stability is now defunct. Education has taken over that role and is now the digger of and the filler in of holes!

While Hoyle objects to what he calls the "meal-ticket aspect" of education (p.52), he emphasises that he is not against education in principle. In fact, he states that it is education which separates the human species from other animals in that the totality of the human experience can be imprinted on one human brain (p.51). He points out that the whole emphasis on education in the formative years of a child's life is misplaced. Children, he rightly says, have an innate linguistic ability between birth and seven years of age, after which the ability to learn languages declines. He also points out that mathematical ability is also prevalent at a very young age. So he believes that it is in these areas that educational policy should make its endeavours in bringing out the best in the intellectual formation of the child. However, he strongly suggests that subjects like History and Literature should not be taught in the formative years, as the child has not, at this age, developed the emotional maturity to understand the way the adult mind works.

Not only does Hoyle see a problem in the earlier stages of education, but at the other end of the spectrum when the child comes to university entrance age. Because students were taught too little of the right things when they were at school, too much is expected of them when they arrive at university (p. 58). Hoyle relates this problem to the current confusion between education and research (p.59). If universities have become "components of popular democracy" (p. 59) then this level of scholastic professionalism which aims to train the future researcher is out of place. While" . . . research needs new recruits who come . . . . from . . . . universities . . . . the appearance in the classroom of the gifted active research worker, is only too likely to lift standards to impossible levels . . . ." (p. 60). Therefore education and research ought to be separated, as the former is simply passing on the totality of the human experience from one generation to the next, whereas the latter is involved in breaking into new and uncharted territory. It represents the "flashes of inspiration" of which Hoyle spoke in his earlier lectures (p.61) He contends that the universities are the best places where research may be conducted for it is only there that the young can criticise the old and challenge long-established ideas and practices. Whereas education has a socio/economic function, research should not have. Rather it should be completely disinterested in its methods of inquiry. For Hoyle, the tragedy is that research "swings along on the coat-tails of education" (p. 62) though it is an essential component in the quest to ensure that ". . . . the whole human species is not to fossilise in its present position" (p.62).

This situation led Hoyle to believe that independent research centres would establish themselves as entities independent of universities. While this has happened to quite a large extent, much research in the first half of the 21st century, is still conducted within the precincts of the university. The complete break between education and research to the extent that it has changed the nature of universities, simply has not occurred. Hoyle did not think that such a break was particularly desirable, his grounds for this being that the place of research within universities was ". . . . an old system which has worked well in the past . . . ." However, he warned that resistance to the minor modifications required in order to achieve these corrective measures would force ". . . . a new system on us" (p.63). Given that research is still very much part of the current university system, it would seem that these modifications have in fact been made.

However, education as a "meal ticket" is a concept which is very much alive and kicking. Once more, we go back to the scene in Chapter 14 of Ms. Pandey's novel to descry the research orientated mind of David in the library. We see a mind purified for research and totally devoid of the "meal-ticket" mentality. Education and research has the same respective distinction as between the material and the abstract, on which Hoyle treated in his opening lecture. It is this latter quality which Ms. Pandey elevates to a higher spiritual level in her novel. That it functions within a human (Mocian) body in Chapter 14 is surely indicative of the higher reaches to which the human mind must aspire if humans are to survive as a species.

✦
✦ ✦

In the final lecture of his series, Sir Fred Hoyle examines the question of the human experience from a much broader philosophical perspective. Quoting from the poet Keats the phrase which states that "the poetry of Earth is never dead," Hoyle admits that while he believes life will not die on Earth, the question as to its poetry ". . . . is under severe threat" (p. 65). The fundamental question uppermost in Hoyle's mind here is the very purpose of the existence of the human species—namely, "what are we doing here?" In attempting to analyse this issue, Hoyle notes that human beings possess a ". . . . curious mixture of nearsightedness and farsightedness" (p. 66). However, most people's preoccupations with the day to day minutiae of life, tend to preclude considerations of this higher question from their thought processes. The basic issue here is one of "motivation" (p. 65). Under certain circumstances human beings can be aroused to this higher level of thinking. Hoyle makes the point that war provides the driving motivational force for the individual to think in terms of community rather than just his own narrow personal self-interest. In the absence of this "directed motivation" (p. 67), it becomes difficult for individuals to work for the benefit of the community; the reason being, that the absence of this directed motivation, creates an "aimless society" (p. 67). Hoyle equates the great achievements of individuals with the general morale of the societies in which they happen to live. Such achievements will fluctuate according to the prevalence or otherwise of favourable circumstances in the societies in which they live. In order to make successful plans for the future, a clearer understanding is required of the ". . . . relationship between the individual and the community . . . ." (p. 68).

In the economic sphere, Hoyle believes we are well-placed to activate such plans, as our present day knowledge of economics is now sufficient to ensure against the vagaries of the circumstances which brought about the Great Depression of the 1930's. Hoyle makes it clear that while we have the ability to successfully plan for things at the institutional, municipal and national levels, we manifestly fail at the international level (ps 65 & 66). He sees this as a general failure of mankind to organise on the largest scale of all. In tackling this question, Hoyle applies the principle often used in science which argues from the postulating of an idealised rather than from an actual experiment. In science, this method of approach often produces fruitful results. (P. 70).

The application of this method to the international scene would involve answering the question, "what would you do if you were given the job of setting things to rights?" (p. 69). Without an adequate answer to this question, it is, according to Hoyle, unfair to place the blame on politicians for the current situation the world now finds itself in. In attempting to answer this profound question, Hoyle looks at the root cause of the problems. He avers that this lies in the environments which prevail in countries—good environments produce good results whist bad environments lead to "animal savagery" (p. 71). In the example he gives of the situation then prevailing in the Congo, Hoyle claims that the lack of organic matter in the soils of Africa is the root cause of the strife so prevalent in that continent. In the wider application of this example, ". . . . nothing can be achieved anywhere on Earth at any time, except through the creation of the appropriate environmental conditions" (p. 71).

In expanding upon the scientific method just referred to above, Hoyle goes on to explain the nature of the approach he takes in dealing with such questions. He argues from what he calls "an axiomatic approach" (p.73) by which he assumes the starting point to be correct. This is in preference to the alternative approach whereby probabilities are attached to the various facets of a situation and, from there, to seek the best balanced description from them. Instead, Hoyle attributes unit probability to the starting point and then accepts the consequences of the deductive argument which comes from that. Hoyle then goes on to apply this method to the issue of human problems and asks "Is there a starting point that we could all agree to adopt and from which everything else would follow by straightforward deduction, . . . ?" (p.73).

Hoyle's starting position is that world organisation cannot be achieved so long as basic ". . . technological and arithmetical issues are made subservient to emotion" (p. 74). Though in reality, emotion tends to win the day, progress cannot be made unless cold logic prevails. The axiomatic example he provides is that children should not be born into a world of misery and hunger. A technological example he gives is in the soils of Africa possessing very little in the way of organic content. The arithmetical example he gives is that as too many children are being born into poverty and misery, population control becomes a necessity.

Yet, it is here that one could argue with Hoyle's axiom—or at least with the solution to it. The reverse argument could be applied by which the proposed solution lies in some form of advance in the agricultural sciences whereby some method is devised to increase the fertility of African soil. Let us say that country A has a population of 40 million and has 50% of its people below the bread-line. And let us further suppose that that country managed to reduce its population to 20 million. The chances are that the percentage figure would not change—instead of 50% of 40 million below the bread-line, there would be 50% of 20 million suffering from this extreme form of poverty. It is also noteworthy that it is the richest countries which have high populations and the poorest which have low populations. It was during the period of the industrial revolution that Britain's population started to increase dramatically. Today, due to its affluence from petrodollars, the Middle Eastern countries are experiencing a boom in their population growth. Japan has a population of over 120 million people and the Philippines has a population of half this amount. Yet, the Philippines is teeming with natural and mineral resources, plus it has good agricultural land. Japan on the other hand is almost devoid of these, yet it is the world's largest economy apart from that of the United States.

It seems then that a more holistic approach to the problem of poverty is required rather than on the concentration of one aspect of it—in this case, overpopulation. And as we have seen, on close analyses (above) population does not really seem to be a problem. In the contrasting examples of Japan and the Philippines just given above, this holistic approach would require the taking of a broader survey embracing the economic practices of both countries— attitude to work, educational policy, corruption and malpractice at governmental level, democratic accountability, agricultural techniques and so forth. By such a close, diligent and detailed study we could deduce why the Philippines, with all its potential in the way of natural endowment, is lagging behind its northern neighbour, which has not been graced so generously by nature. In bringing this argument to a conclusion, we can say that there is no evidence, either historical or contemporary, which equates low population with prosperity or high population with poverty—in fact the opposite seems to be the case.

In the final part of his lecture, Hoyle elucidates how he envisages the situation during the last part of the 20th century and the first part of the 21st. "I would hope that as the twenty-first century opens, the present muddles of world organisation might be on their way to a solution" (p. 76). As we are now past the first decade of the new century, we see little evidence that man has improved on his ability to organise any more effectively on a global scale. The conflicts around the globe are as numerous as before, and the United Nations has proven to be completely ineffective in dealing with them.

Hoyle's other prediction involves a higher standard of living and more machines. In this he seems to be correct, especially in terms of the new digital and micro-chip technology. However, he did not see anything very positive in this sort of development, as humanity's sense of purpose would be lost and that civilization would ". . . . degenerate

into a 'biological noise' . . . ." Hoyle then categorically states that
". . . the poetry of the Earth would then indeed be dead" (p. 77). If
such things as poverty and hunger are eliminated, then boredom and
monotony would become the main enemies as humanity would then
lack any sense of purpose for the reason that "both the material and
spiritual aims of life are in retreat, ..." (p. 78). It is here that man will
have to rediscover the spiritual values which have always been his
raison d'etre. Perhaps there will be a paradigm shift from the material
to the spiritual. However, in the modern world of PCs, iphones and
such like things, there is very little in the way of evidence that this is in
any sense currently happening. In education and research, we still ask
the material question "what is the use of it?"

Physics provides a flicker of the spiritual as scientists seek a
Grand Unified Theory of Everything. Hoyle, however, doubts that "an
ultimate understanding" of nature will come about. Since 1966, when
Hoyle delivered these lectures, we have discovered the Higgs Boson
particle. However, this particle's discovery may pose more questions
than it answers. Hoyle explained that the major discoveries of every
age appeared to give the impression of "ultimate understanding."
He doubted that we would ever come to what he called this "level of
sophistication" for to do so would mean that our brains and intellectual
abilities are precisely matched to the external world around us. It is
this which may be mankind's saving grace, for however much we
discover in the way of scientific inquiry, the Universe will never yield all
its secrets; nature will only provide tid bits every now and again.

"In the second chapter I said that the laws of physics, the laws
which prescribe 'the game,' represent the modern extrapolation of
the concept of God" (p. 79). However various religions and belief
systems view God, one thing we can be sure of is that we will have to
abandon the idea of "what is the use of it?" and start researching and
investigating the nature of reality for the sheer sake of it. Hoyle avers
that when the material requirements of the species have been met,
"abstract curiosity" will have to ". . . stand in its own right" (p. 80).

In fact, the more we delve into the strange world of quantum
mechanics, the closer we come to a realisation of how the material
and the spiritual/abstract overlap with one another—in physics, we
may say, the close connection between physics and metaphysics.
Hoyle's prediction of this value change still has to come about. In 2014

(at the time of writing) we are still overawed by machines, we are still asking the question as to the "use" of things, and we still eschew the noble concepts of the abstract and the spiritual—the notion of inquiry for inquiry's sake being quite alien to the thought processes of our culture.

By basing her characters on spirit beings, Aishwarya Pandey seems to have captured the currently dormant spiritual aspects of mankind. The "forbidden book" may well be a metaphor of the deep and penetrating questions that still somehow manage to surface through the thick layers of materialism that mankind has buried itself in throughout its eons of technological development. We may never be able to actually steal this book, but we are able to grab, at times, a few of its sentences, paragraphs and even pages. But the book is a massive volume, Nature's devotional work of spirituality which never finds its ultimate conclusion.